MONSTERS AMONG US:

TERRIFYINGLY TRUE SASQUATCH & DOGMAN ENCOUNTERS

LUKA T. JACOBS

DEDICATION

As always, thank you to my family
for their unwavering support.

CONTENTS

NOTE FROM THE AUTHOR

Thank you for choosing my book, a collection of true and horrifying encounters with Sasquatch and Dogman submitted by brave individuals from across the United States and Canada. Each story within these pages recounts an experience that has left an indelible mark on the person who lived it. These are not mere campfire tales or urban legends; they are genuine accounts of encounters with cryptids, shared by those who have faced the inexplicable and lived to tell the tale.

The stories you will read have been carefully edited for clarification, flow, and grammar to ensure they capture the essence of each encounter while providing a seamless reading experience. I have taken great care to preserve the authenticity and raw emotion of each submission, respecting the courage it took for each person to come forward and share their experience.

Throughout this journey, you will hear from people

from all walks of life—retired state troopers, hunters, hikers, and everyday citizens—who found themselves face-to-face with creatures that defy logic and challenge our understanding of the natural world. Their stories are gripping, suspenseful, and often terrifying, where myth becomes reality.

This collection is not just about fear; it is about curiosity, survival, and the human spirit's resilience in the face of the unknown. As you read, I encourage you to keep an open mind and remember that the world is vast and filled with mysteries that we are only beginning to understand.

Thank you for joining me on this exploration of the extraordinary. I hope these stories will leave you as fascinated and haunted as they have left me.

Happy reading!

Luka. T. Jacobs

As always, feel free to reach out or keep up to date with upcoming books via my FB page https://www.facebook.com/lukatjacobs or my website https://www.lukatjacobs.com.

IT FOLLOWED ME

GEORGIA

The Appalachian Trail had always called to me, a whisper in the winds of the mountains, a challenge to my spirit. I'd read about the vast stretches of untouched wilderness, the serenity of the rolling hills, and the camaraderie of the trail's community. So, when the chance finally came to hike it alone, I seized it with both hands. Little did I know, this journey would not just test my endurance, but push the boundaries of my sanity.

I started in Georgia, standing at the foot of Springer Mountain. The weather was clear, the air crisp with the early signs of spring. The trail ahead seemed endless, a ribbon of earth winding through the heart of the Appalachian Mountains. I was prepared for solitude, for long days of walking and nights spent under a canopy of stars. What I wasn't prepared for was the relentless presence that would shadow my every step.

The first few days were blissful. I fell into a rhythm, my feet crunching over the path, my eyes drinking in the beauty of the wildflowers and the vibrant greenery. The trail was challenging, but I relished the physical exertion, the sweat on my brow, the burn in my muscles. I met a few hikers along the way, exchanged pleasantries, and sometimes shared a campfire. But mostly, I was alone, just as I had hoped.

It was on the fifth day that I first sensed something was off. The trail had taken me deeper into the woods, where the trees grew taller and closer together, their branches forming a thick canopy overhead. The light was dim, and the air was heavy with the scent of pine and damp earth. I was about fifteen miles from the nearest town, and the isolation was complete.

I was walking at a steady pace, my thoughts lost in the rhythm of my footsteps, when I heard it—a faint rustling behind me. I stopped, turning to scan the woods, but saw nothing unusual. The forest was silent, save for the occasional chirp of a bird or the rustle of leaves in the breeze. I shrugged it off and continued, but I didn't feel alone.

As the day wore on, the feeling grew stronger. I couldn't shake the sensation that I was being watched, that unseen eyes were tracking my every move. I quickened my pace, my heart beating a little faster. The trail twisted and turned, and I found myself glancing over my shoulder more frequently, each time expecting to see something in the shadows. But there was nothing—only the trees and the silence.

By late afternoon, I decided to make camp. I found a small clearing off the trail, surrounded by dense thickets. It was a good spot, sheltered and hidden from view. I set up my tent, gathered some wood, and started a fire. The flames danced and crackled, casting long shadows that flickered across the trees.

As I sat by the fire, cooking my dinner, the feeling of being watched intensified. The woods around me seemed to close in, the darkness between the trees growing deeper. I ate quickly, my eyes constantly darting to the edge of the clearing. The rustling noise came again, louder this time, and I stood up, shining my flashlight into the woods.

"Hello?" I called out, my voice sounding small and uncertain. "Is anyone there?"

Silence. I swept the beam of the flashlight back and forth, but saw nothing. The hair on the back of my neck stood up, and I felt a chill run down my spine. I backed towards the fire, my hand gripping the flashlight tightly. I knew I was alone out here—or at least, I thought I was.

After a while, the sounds stopped, and the forest returned to its usual stillness. I tried to shake off the fear, convincing myself it was just an animal—a deer, maybe, or a raccoon. I stoked the fire, adding more wood, and forced myself to relax. I couldn't let my imagination get the best of me. I was out here to enjoy myself and I was doing a bad job at it.

As the night deepened, I crawled into my tent, zipping it up securely. I lay on my sleeping bag, staring at the roof of the tent, listening to the crackling of the fire outside. Gradually, the warmth and the rhythmic sounds lulled me to sleep.

I don't know how long I slept, but I woke with a start, my heart skipping beats. The fire had died down to embers, casting a faint, eerie glow. I lay still, straining to hear. There it was again—that damn rustling sound, closer this time, accompanied by the soft crunch of footsteps on leaves. Someone—or something—was circling my campsite.

I held my breath, my senses on high alert. The footsteps stopped, replaced by a deep, heavy breathing. It was right outside my tent. I could hear the sound of it inhaling and exhaling, slow and it clearly meant for me to hear it. What was this thing? It didn't sound like any animal I knew of. It was too intelligent to be a bear and the breathing sounded like something with a massive lung capacity.

For a moment, I was paralyzed with fear. The breathing continued, a steady, rhythmic sound that seemed to grow louder. I thought I was going to lose control of my bodily functions any minute. I reached for my flashlight, my hand shaking. Slowly, I unzipped the tent just enough to peer outside.

The beam of light pierced the darkness, but all I saw

were the trees and the glowing embers of the fire. The breathing stopped abruptly, and the silence was deafening. I scanned the clearing, my flashlight flicking back and forth, but saw nothing. I was so scared I could feel my pulse in my ears.

I zipped the tent back up, and got back into my sleeping bag. What the hell was out there? I lay back down, gripping the flashlight like a lifeline. I didn't sleep much the rest of the night, my ears straining for any sound, my mind conjuring up images of what could be out there in the shadows.

When dawn finally broke, I was exhausted but relieved. The light of day made the fear seem almost irrational. I packed up my camp quickly, eager to put distance between myself and whatever had haunted me during the night. I resumed my hike, my pace quicker than usual, driven by a lingering unease.

The day passed without incident, but it still felt like I was being followed. The trail took me even deeper into the forest, the trees growing thicker, the light dimmer. I was constantly watching my back.

As evening approached, I found another clearing to set up camp. It was smaller than the previous one, more enclosed by trees. I built a fire, more out of a need for comfort than warmth, and cooked a quick meal. The forest around me was quiet, too quiet, and the sense of unease grew stronger.

I sat by the fire, staring into the flames, my mind replaying the events of the previous night. The rustling, the footsteps, the breathing—it had all felt so real. I couldn't shake the feeling that I was being hunted, that something out there was watching me, waiting.

As night fell, the sounds started again. This time, they were closer, more purposeful. I sat up, gripping the flashlight and a small camping knife. The fire cast flickering shadows, making the trees seem to move and shift. I strained to see, to hear, every sense working overtime.

The footsteps circled my camp, slow and calculated. I could hear the crunch of leaves, the snap of twigs. The breathing came again, deep and heavy, making my skin crawl. I shone the flashlight into the darkness, but it revealed nothing. The creature—whatever it was—stayed just out of sight, hidden in the shadows. It was smart and it felt like it was just toying with me.

I sat there for what felt like hours, every nerve in my body on edge. The sounds continued, relentless and terrifying. I could feel my sanity slipping, the fear consuming me. The creature seemed to know exactly how to unsettle me, how to keep me on the brink of panic.

At some point, the sounds stopped. The silence was almost worse, the anticipation of what might happen next. I didn't dare move, didn't dare make a sound. I just sat there, gripping the flashlight and the knife, my eyes wide and unblinking.

Eventually, exhaustion overtook me, and I must have

dozed off. I woke with a start, the dawn light filtering through the trees. I was stiff and sore, my mind a fog of fear and fatigue. I packed up my camp quickly, my hands shaking. I needed to get out of there, to find some semblance of safety.

I can't remember much of the hike that day. I moved quickly, my eyes darting to every shadow, every movement. The feeling of being followed, a constant presence at the edge of my awareness. I didn't stop to eat, didn't stop to rest. I just kept moving, driven by a primal fear.

As evening approached, I found myself in a more open area, the trees thinning out. I decided to set up camp, hoping that the openness would offer some protection. I built a fire, more out of habit than anything else, and tried to eat, but the food turned to ash in my mouth.

The night was quiet at first, but I knew better than to let my guard down. I sat by the fire, my senses once again working overtime. The rustling started again, the footsteps, the breathing. This time, it was different—more aggressive, more menacing. The creature was getting bolder.

I shone the flashlight into the darkness, my heart pounding. The beam of light caught a glimpse of something—eyes, glowing red, staring back at me. I gasped, stumbling back, the flashlight shaking in my hand.

The eyes disappeared, but my fear increased. I could hear it circling, moving closer. The firelight flickered, casting eerie shadows. The breathing was louder, more pronounced. I felt trapped, surrounded, with no escape.

I backed up to my tent, my hand gripping the knife so tightly my knuckles turned white. The sounds grew louder, the presence more oppressive. I could feel eyes on me, feel its intent. It was playing with me.

I don't know how long I stood there, every muscle tense, every sense buzzing with anticipation. Time seemed to stretch, every second an eternity. The creature moved in the shadows, just out of sight, its presence a constant fear.

At some point, I must have passed out from sheer exhaustion. I abruptly awakened, the morning light filtering through the trees, once again. I was on the ground, the fire reduced to embers. My body ached, my mind turned to mush.

I packed up my camp quickly, every movement filled with a sense of urgency. I needed to get out of there, back to civilization. I resumed my hike, my pace quick and determined.

The trail eventually led me to a small town. I stumbled into the first diner I saw, my appearance haggard and wild. The patrons stared at me, their conversations stopping mid-sentence. I must have looked like a madman, disheveled and haunted.

I sat down at a table, my hands shaking. I ordered food and ate mechanically, the taste barely registering. The other patrons whispered among themselves, their eyes darting towards me.

I stayed in that town for a few days, as it felt so much safer to do so. The memory of those eyes, those sounds, haunted my every waking moment. I couldn't bring myself to return to the trail, to face whatever was out there.

Eventually, I made my way back home, disappointed that my dream hadn't turned out the way I had hoped.

To this day, I can't fully explain what happened to me on the Appalachian Trail. But I know one thing for certain—I'll never set foot in those woods again. The fear, the terror, the sense of being hunted—it's something I wouldn't wish on anyone.

NIGHT AT THE ROADHOUSE

My name is Huck and I've been a trucker for over twenty years. Born and raised in Idaho, I've driven these roads more times than I can count. I've seen my fair share of weird things out there, but nothing quite like what happened one chilly November night at a roadhouse just off Highway 95.

I was hauling a load of potatoes down to Boise and decided to pull over for the night. The roadhouse was a popular spot for truckers—a small diner with a big parking lot, always a few rigs parked overnight. I found a spot near the back, turned off the engine, and settled in for some much-needed shut-eye.

The night was clear, and the air had a bite to it, a reminder that winter was here. The parking lot was quieter than usual, with only a few other trucks scattered around. I closed my eyes and tried to drift off, but for some reason, sleep wouldn't come. After tossing and turning for what felt like hours, I finally gave up and decided to get out and have a smoke.

I stepped out of the cab and lit up a cigarette, the ember glowing bright in the dark. The night was eerily quiet, not a sound except for the occasional rustle of leaves in the wind. It was spooky, to be honest, like the calm before a storm. I looked around, seeing the dark shapes of the other trucks silhouetted against the dim glow of the roadhouse's neon sign.

Something didn't feel right, but I couldn't put my finger on it. I don't get spooked easily, so I took a deep drag and tried to shake off the unease, chalking it up to being overtired. After a few minutes, I finished my cigarette, flicked the butt away, and climbed back into the truck. I laid back down, hoping sleep would come easier this time.

It couldn't have been more than twenty minutes later when I was jolted awake by a strange noise. It was a scraping sound, like something dragging across metal, followed by a blowing noise, almost like a deer makes. My heart started pounding in my chest, and I strained to listen. The noise stopped for a moment, then started up again, louder this time.

I sat up in my bunk, peering out the window. The parking lot was dark, and I couldn't see much beyond the dim glow of the diner. The noise continued, scraping and blowing, unnerving me. I'd never heard anything like it before.

Out of my peripheral vision I saw movement between the trucks. At first, I thought it was a wolf, but something was seriously off. It was walking on two legs, hunched over, and had hands similar to a raccoons. It's lower body was skinny but the top half looked like it was pure muscle.

I could only see it from the back, but it was enough to make my blood pressure sky rocket. It was slightly hunched as it sniffed the air, then it headed towards another truck parked a few spaces away.

Is that a freakin' werewolf, I thought.

My brain whirled, attempting to process the sight before me. It looked like a wolf, but wolves don't walk on two legs. I watched in horror as it reached the other truck, disappearing into the shadows. The blowing noise came again, louder and more insistent.

I wanted to get out of there, to start the engine and drive away as fast as I could, but I didn't want it to notice me. I couldn't move, couldn't think. All I could do was sit there, heart pounding, eyes fixed on the spot where the creature had disappeared.

I am 55 years old and nothing has ever terrified me like that creature did.

After a while, the noise stopped. The night was silent again, and I tried to calm my breathing. I laid back down, pulling the blanket up to my chin, ears straining for any sound. I don't know how long I lay there, tense and trembling, but eventually, exhaustion took over, and I drifted off to sleep.

I woke up to the harsh light of morning, the events of the night before feeling like a bad dream. But the unease was still there, a lingering sense of dread that wouldn't go away. I climbed out of the truck, looking around the parking lot. Everything seemed normal, but I couldn't shake the feeling that something was watching me.

I quickly did my pre-trip inspection, eager to get back on the road and put as much distance between me and that roadhouse as possible. As I pulled out of the lot, I vowed never to stop there again. Whatever that thing was, I didn't want to see it again.

In the days and weeks that followed, I couldn't stop thinking about that night. I tried to rationalize it, to convince myself that it was just my imagination, that I was overtired and seeing things. But deep down, I knew what I had seen was real. The memory of that creature, walking on two legs, its eerie movements, haunted me.

I dared to mention my sighting to a few other truckers, but most of them just laughed it off, thinking I was joking around. One old-timer though, stopped me as I was leaving and simply said "what you saw was real".

I was a bit taken aback, but glad I wasn't the only one that had seen this evil-looking creature. .

THE FACE UNDER THE PORCH

I've got to tell you a story that's been haunting me for years. My name's Jason, and I'm 26 now, living in Vancouver. I moved here after college, wanting to put some distance between myself and the place where this story takes place. My parents have a rural property outside of Kamloops, BC, and I've hated it ever since we moved there when I was 15. I never could quite explain why—it just never felt right to me. My parents, though, they absolutely love the place.

Recently, I decided it was time for my girlfriend, Emily, to meet my folks. She'd been curious about my reluctance to visit my childhood home and why I seemed uneasy whenever it came up in conversation. I thought maybe facing it head-on would help, so we flew into Kamloops, hired a car, and started the drive out to the property. It was around 7 PM in early May, with the sun just dipping below the horizon.

As we pulled down the long gravel driveway, I felt that familiar knot of unease tighten in my stomach. The driveway was flanked by tall trees on either side, and the house sat at the end like an island of refuge—or, in my case, a place of dread. My parents had installed a motion-operated light on the front porch, but it didn't do much to cut through the encroaching darkness. I even commented to Emily about how useless that light was, trying to mask my nerves with a bit of humor.

We parked and got out of the car. I grabbed Emily's hand, partly for comfort and partly to reassure her. As we walked towards the porch, I stopped suddenly. There was something under the porch, just at the edge of the dim light. I pulled Emily back towards the car quickly, my heart pounding.

"What's wrong?" she asked, her voice tinged with confusion and concern.

"Just get in the car," I said, trying to keep my voice steady. We climbed back in, and I backed up the driveway, not taking my eyes off the porch.

Once we were a safe distance away, Emily demanded to know what had happened. I took a deep breath and tried to calm down before explaining. "When I got closer to the porch, I saw a face under there. At first, I thought it was just a dog or something, but then it grinned at me—like an evil Joker's grin, all teeth and malice. It was like a wolf's face, but not quite. It had this sinister look in its eyes. It's face was pure evil."

Emily looked at me, her eyes wide. "Are you sure it wasn't just a neighbor's dog or something?"

I shook my head. "No way. It was too large and I have never seen a dog look like that thing before. It is like it wanted me to see it and it wanted me to be terrified. I don't know how I know that but I do."

I called my parents from the road and told them what I saw. They were angry and brushed it off, insisting it was probably just a neighbor's dog. I wasn't convinced and refused to go back. We agreed to meet in town at a restaurant instead. Over dinner, I tried to convince them to move, but they were adamant about staying.

The rest of the trip was uneventful, but that encounter refuses to leave my mind. I will never go back to that property.

Emily believed me, and we talked about it here and there, trying to make sense of what I'd seen. To this day, my parents still live there, but I've never set foot on that land again. There's something out there, something that doesn't want me around, and I'm more than happy to oblige.

TERROR AT THE CABIN

WASHINGTON

Growing up, my brother Craig and I shared a love for the great outdoors. Our childhood was filled with camping trips, fishing adventures, and exploring the forests near our home in the Pacific Northwest. As we got older, our busy lives often kept us apart, but we always tried to make time for our annual fishing trip. This year, we decided to rent a cabin in a remote part of the woods, far away from the hustle and bustle of our everyday lives.

I remember pretty much every detail of this trip and will relay it to the best of my ability.

The cabin was a quaint little place, nestled deep in the forest, surrounded by towering pine trees and a serene lake. It was perfect for our needs—no cell service, no distractions, just us, the wilderness, and plenty of fish to catch. We arrived on a sunny afternoon, the drive long but scenic. The smell of pine and earth was invigorating. Just what we needed.

Craig and I spent the first day settling in, unpacking our gear, and exploring the area around the cabin. We found a good spot by the lake for fishing, set up our rods, and spent the evening reminiscing about our childhood adventures. As the sun set, we made our way back to the cabin, a successful day of fishing behind us.

The cabin was cozy, with a small living area, a kitchenette, and one bedroom with two bunks. We made a fire in the fireplace, cooked a hearty dinner, and enjoyed a few beers. The isolation was refreshing, a welcome break from our hectic lives. As the night grew darker, the forest around us came alive with the sounds of nocturnal creatures. We turned in early, eager for another day of fishing.

I woke up in the middle of the night to a strange sound. At first, I thought it was just the wind through the trees, but as I listened more closely, I realized it was something else. It sounded like heavy footsteps slowly moving around the cabin. I started feeling a little anxious, and I strained to hear more.

The footsteps were louder now, circling the cabin. Craig and I exchanged a worried glance. Maybe it was a bear, but the footsteps were too heavy, too pronounced, and clearly bipedal. It didn't make sense for someone to come all this way just to be playing a prank on us or try to scare us.

We each got out of our beds and crept to the window, peering out into the darkness. We couldn't see anything, but the footsteps continued, moving around the cabin. This was getting too creepy. We grabbed flashlights and weapons—a baseball bat and a hunting knife—and moved cautiously to the door.

As we stepped out onto the porch the footsteps stopped, and the silence was almost deafening. We shone our flashlights into the woods, but saw nothing. The forest was still, the only sound our own breathing. Something was toying with us, and it didn't seem like some dumb animal, it seemed intelligent.

We stood there for a few more minutes, but the footsteps didn't return. Reluctantly, we went back inside, locking the door behind us. We sat by the fireplace, too on edge to go back to sleep. We stayed up for the rest of the night, expecting something to happen. But the footsteps didn't return, and eventually, the first light of dawn began to filter through the trees. We were exhausted, but the daylight brought a sense of relief.

We spent the next day fishing, trying to shake off the fear from the night before. The lake was calm, the fish plentiful, and for a while, we managed to relax. As evening approached, we made our way back to the cabin. We cooked dinner, but the mood was tense. Every creak of the cabin set our nerves on edge. We tried to distract ourselves with card games and more beers, but it wasn't working very well.

That night, the footsteps returned. I woke up to the sound of heavy breathing right outside my window. My heart felt like it would explode, but I laid still. What the hell was out there? Craig woke up, his face pale in the moonlight. He asked what we should do and I said just to stay calm and lets slowly check it out.

We crept to the window, peering out into the darkness. The breathing was much louder now. I shone my flashlight outside, and for a moment, I thought I saw something— two glowing eyes, staring back at me. I gasped, stumbling back, the flashlight shaking in my hand.

I told Craig and he grabbed his baseball bat, his grip tight. I said lets check it out. We moved to the door, our flashlights cutting through the darkness. The breathing stopped abruptly, and the silence was almost worse.

We stepped outside, the cold night air biting at our skin. We shone our flashlights around, but saw nothing. The forest was still, and we didn't hear a sound. But I could feel it—something had its eyes on us. Craig wondered if it was a bear and I said it wasn't acting like any bear I've seen or heard of.

We stood there for what felt like hours, every muscle tense, every sense on overdrive. The breathing started again, closer this time. I shone my flashlight towards the sound, and for a brief moment, I saw it—a massive, hulking humanoid figure, standing at the edge of the trees. It was covered in dark hair, its eyes glowing red in the moonlight. *What the hell is that*, I thought.

We both stared, glued to the spot, as the creature stepped closer. It was huge. I am not great with heights but I'd be guessing anywhere from 8 to 9 feet tall, shoulders like a footballer and the arms on this thing were insane. It moved so smoothly, its eyes never leaving us.

We backed towards the cabin, our eyes never leaving the creature. It watched us, its breathing heavy and menacing. As we reached the door, it stopped, standing at the edge of the clearing. We slammed the door shut, locking it tightly.

We sat by the fireplace, staring into the fire. We stayed up for the rest of the night, hoping it would just leave us alone. As the first light of dawn began to filter through the trees the tension eased just slightly.

We decided to stay close to the cabin that day, too afraid to venture far. We gathered wood, made sure the cabin was secure, and kept our eyes on the forest. The daylight brought some comfort, but we couldn't relax knowing this thing was around.

Being as stubborn as we are, neither of us wanted to admit we should leave. I wish we had.

As evening approached, the tension grew once again. We cooked dinner, but ate in silence, every noise setting our nerves on edge. The forest around us grew darker, the shadows deeper. We knew the creature would return.

That night, the creature startled us by slapping the outside of the cabin so hard that my glass of water on the bedside table spilled. We both jumped out of our beds, standing in the middle of the room, shaking like crazy

The creature then circled the cabin, its footsteps echoing in the stillness. We could hear it moving, its presence a constant, oppressive force. I shone my flashlight out the window, but saw nothing. The creature stayed just out of sight, hidden in the shadows.

The hours passed by slowly, every minute dragging on. We felt so vulnerable against such a formidable creature.

At some point, I must have dozed off. I woke when the sun was already up. The creature was gone, but our anxiety remained.

I told Craig I couldn't do another night there. I was exhausted and so was he. We packed up our gear quickly, our eyes constantly on the forest.

We loaded up the car, every movement filled with urgency. As we drove away, the cabin growing smaller in the rearview mirror, I felt a sense of relief. We didn't speak much on the drive back, both of us lost in our thoughts.

When we finally reached home, I went over the nights at the cabin in my head, trying to make it make sense. The thought that it was a Bigfoot seemed too fantastical, too unbelievable. But I knew what we had experienced, and it had felt all too real.

Later, I did leave a review that there was a large animal on the property. I hoped that whoever stayed there after us didn't have the same experience.

HIGHWAY TERROR

OREGON

I've been drivin' trucks for nigh on thirty years now, and I thought I'd seen just about everything the road could throw at me. I've hauled loads through blizzards in Montana, crossed the scorching deserts of Arizona, and navigated the tightest city streets you can imagine. But nothin', and I mean nothin', prepared me for what happened one late summer night on a lonely stretch of highway in the Pacific Northwest.

I'm Jeb, born and raised in a small town in Georgia. Truck drivin' is in my blood—my daddy did it, and his daddy before him. I've got stories that'd make your hair stand on end, but this one, well, this one still keeps me up at night.

I was haulin' a load of timber out of Oregon, headin'

south to California. The sun had long since dipped below the horizon, and the sky was pitch black, save for the occasional glimmer of stars. It was one of those nights where the air felt thick with anticipation. The kind of night where you keep your headlights on high beam and your eyes peeled for deer dartin' out from the woods.

I had my old dog, Max, ridin' shotgun with me. Max was a faithful companion, a grizzled old hound who'd been with me for years. He was gettin' on in age, but he still had a keen sense for trouble. If something was off, Max would know it and I trusted him more than I trusted myself.

We were makin' good time, the engine's gentle growl and the tires' repetitive tap on the pavement brought me into a comfortable rhythm. The highway was deserted, not another soul in sight. Just me, my rig, Max, and the endless stretch of road ahead. It was my happy place.

It must've been around midnight when I first got that feelin'. You know the one—when the hairs on the back of your neck stand up and a cold shiver runs down your spine. I couldn't put my finger on it, but somethin' just felt…off. I glanced at the clock on the dashboard, watchin' the seconds tick by, tryin' to shake the unease settlin' in my gut.

Max started growlin' low in his throat, his ears perked up and his eyes fixed on the road ahead. That dog had a sixth sense for danger, and if he was uneasy, then I knew somethin' was wrong.

I was coming up on a bend in the road, my headlights

cutting through the darkness, when I saw it. At first, I thought my eyes were playing tricks on me, or some idiot was out there hitchhiking and about to get hit. But there, in the middle of the road, stood a tall, broad figure, silhouetted against the night. I slowed down, squinting to get a better look.

As I got closer, my heart skipped a beat. This wasn't no deer, no bear, hell, it wasn't even a person. It was somethin' else entirely. The figure stood at least eight, maybe nine feet tall, with long hair coverin' its body. Its arms hung low, almost reachin' its knees, and its eyes glowed a deep, menacing red in the glare of my headlights.

I slammed on the brakes, my rig screechin' to a halt. The thing didn't move, just stood there, starin' at me. For a moment, we were locked in a silent standoff, the engine idlin' beneath me and my heart hammerin' in my chest.

Max was barkin' now, a deep, fierce sound that echoed in the cab. I'd never heard this sound from him before. I grabbed my gun from under the seat, my hands shakin', but I stayed put. There was no way in hell I was gettin' out of that truck.

The creature didn't move, just watched me with those red eyes. It was massive, its presence fillin' the air with a sense of dread. I could feel the fear settlin' in my bones, but I wasn't about to let it control me.

"Hey!" I shouted through the closed window, my voice muffled by the glass. "Get outta here!"

The creature tilted its head, almost as if it was considerin' my words. Then, with a low growl, it turned and loped off the road, headin' toward a steep cliff that rose up from the side of the highway. I watched in stunned silence as it scaled the rock face with ease, disappearin' into the shadows.

I sat there for a moment, my heart skippin' beats. I'd heard stories of Bigfoot, sure—who hasn't? Just stories to scare the kids, I thought. Yet, that is exactly what I saw, there was no mistaking it.

I finally managed to get my rig movin' again, my mind going a million miles an hour. I kept my eyes on the road, but my thoughts were a jumbled mess. What the hell had I just seen? And more importantly, what was it doin' out here?

The rest of the drive was a blur. I kept glancin' in my mirrors, half expectin' to see those red eyes starin' back at me. By the time I reached the truck stop where I'd planned to rest for the night, I was a bundle of nerves. I parked my rig, shut off the engine, and just sat there, tryin' to calm down.

Max had settled down, but he kept lookin' out the window, his ears twitchin' every now and then. I didn't sleep much that night. Every time I closed my eyes, I saw that creature, its hulkin' form and those eerie, glowin' eyes. I lay in my bunk, listenin' to the sounds of the truck stop, tryin' to convince myself it had all been a bad dream. But deep down, I knew better.

The next mornin', I hit the road again, tryin' to put as many miles between me and that stretch of highway as possible. But no matter how far I drove, every shadow by the side of the road made my heart race.

I stopped at a diner for breakfast, hopin' a hot meal would steady my nerves. The waitress, a friendly woman named Betty, noticed my jittery state and asked if I was alright. I hesitated, wonderin' if I should tell her what I'd seen. In the end, I decided against it. Who'd believe me, anyway?

Months passed, and I did my best to move on. But that night haunted me, a shadow I couldn't shake. I started takin' different routes, avoidin' that stretch of highway like the plague. I didn't want to see that creature again, didn't want to feel that fear.

Years have passed since that night, but the memory is as vivid as ever. I still drive trucks, still haul loads across the country, but now I say a prayer before every trip.

PAW PAW'S STORY

KENTUCKY

Howdy, y'all. The name's Richard, and I've got a story that's been passed down from my Paw Paw that still makes my hair stand on end every time I think about it. Paw Paw was 30 years old when this happened, living on the old family property out in Kentucky. Now, he was a no-nonsense kind of man, but this tale always left him with a haunted look in his eyes.

It was a chilly fall morning, and Paw Paw had gotten up early, as he always did, to have his coffee before the sun came up. The first hints of dawn were just startin' to creep over the horizon. He went to sit on his porch, enjoying the peaceful quiet of the morning, the kind that makes you feel at one with the world.

As he was sippin' his coffee, he heard something that made him sit up straight. It was the sound of a baby cryin', comin' from down by the creek. Now, Paw Paw had neighbors, but they weren't that close, and this sound was too near for comfort. It was a haunting, gut-wrenching cry that sent a chill right down to his bones.

He sat there, listenin', tryin' to make sense of it. His heart was beatin' faster, and he felt a mix of worry and curiosity. The sound was so out of place, so wrong, that he couldn't just ignore it. But bein' a cautious man, he decided to go back inside and grab his shotgun, just to be safe.

With the shotgun in hand, he headed down towards the creek, followin' the cryin' sound. The closer he got, the sicker he felt. It was like his stomach was tied up in knots, and he started to feel a deep sense of dread. He was about to turn back when he saw movement between two bushes.

What he saw next nearly made him trip over his own feet. There, crouched down between the bushes, was a black wolf. But this was no ordinary wolf. It was making the baby crying sound, and it looked like it was mixed with a hyena. Its fur was matted and patchy, like it had mange. The creature's eyes were cold and sinister, and it gave off a sense of malevolence that Paw Paw had never felt before.

The sight of that thing made his blood run cold. He was so shocked and scared that he forgot all about the shotgun in his hands. All he could think about was gettin' away from there as fast as he could. He turned and ran back to the house not stopping until he was back inside with the door shut tight behind him.

Paw Paw never saw that creature again, and he was damn glad about it. He was a tough man, not easily scared, but that morning left him shaken to his core. He told the story many times, always with the same haunted look in his eyes, and it always creeped the hell out of me when he did.

He never did figure out what that creature was or why it was making that awful baby cryin' sound. Some folks said it was a skinwalker, others thought it might be some kind of evil spirit. But whatever it was, it was somethin' that didn't belong in our world.

As I sit here, tellin' y'all this story, I can still see Paw Paw's face, lined with age and wisdom, his eyes filled with the memory of that terrifying encounter. It's a story that's become part of our family's lore, a reminder that there are things out there that we can't explain, things that can shake even the strongest of men.

So, if you ever find yourself out in the Kentucky woods early in the mornin', and you hear the sound of a baby cryin', think twice before you go investigatin'. There are somethin's out there that are better left alone.

That's Paw Paw's story, folks, and I imagine it gives y'all the chills just like it does me every time I hear it.

THE FISHERMAN'S ENCOUNTER

Life in Alaska can be as beautiful as it is harsh. The sprawling wilderness, the biting cold, and the stark beauty of the landscape are part of what makes this place home. My name is JC, and I've spent my entire life in the small fishing town of Kodiak. There are stories you hear growing up in Alaska, stories of things lurking in the woods, but I never put much stock in them—until I saw it for myself, that is.

I've been a fisherman for as long as I can remember. My father taught me the trade, and his father before him. Out here, the sea is both a lifeline and a challenge. The work is tough, but it's honest, and it's all I've ever known. It was late August, and the salmon run was in full swing. The days were long, and the nights were just starting to grow cooler, hinting at the coming fall.

On that particular day, I had decided to fish one of my favorite spots, a secluded inlet a few miles from town. It's a bit of a trek, but it's worth it for the solitude and the bounty of fish. The morning was cool and refreshing, the sky a brilliant shade of blue. I loaded up my gear and set out, the gravel road crunching under the tires of my old pickup truck.

The drive to the inlet took about an hour, the road winding through dense forests and along the rugged coastline. I parked my truck in a small clearing and made my way down the narrow trail to the water's edge. The inlet was just as I remembered it—calm, peaceful, and teeming with fish. I set up my gear and got to work, casting my line and settling into the familiar rhythm of fishing.

The hours passed quickly, the sun climbing higher in the sky. I was having a good day, the fish practically jumping onto my line. The only sounds were the gentle lapping of the water, the distant call of a bald eagle, and the occasional splash of a fish breaking the surface. It was perfect.

As the afternoon wore on, I noticed the forest around me growing quieter. The usual sounds of birds and small animals seemed to fade away, creating a haunting stillness. I brushed it off at first, chalking it up to my imagination. But then I felt it—and my hair stood up all over my body.

I scanned the tree line, my eyes searching for any sign of movement. The forest was dense, the trees standing tall and close together, their branches creating a thick canopy overhead. I couldn't see anything out of the ordinary, but the feeling persisted.

Trying to shake off the unease, I turned my attention back to my fishing. I was in the middle of reeling in a particularly feisty salmon when I heard it—a fierce, throaty rumble that scared the crap outta me. I stood still, my heart beating furiously. The growl came again, louder this time, and I slowly turned to face the forest.

There, standing at the edge of the trees, was a creature unlike anything I'd ever seen. It was massive, easily eight feet tall, covered in thick, auburn/brown hair. Its shoulders were broad, and its arms almost reached its knees. The creature's eyes were black, and it stared at me with an intensity that made my blood run cold.

For a moment, I was seized by fear. My mind buzzed, trying to make sense of what I was seeing. This couldn't be real. But it was. The creature took a step to the side, and I could see the muscles rippling beneath its hair. It was powerful, and it was interested in me.

My instincts kicked in, and I put my hands up and slowly backed away, keeping my eyes on the creature. My fishing gear lay forgotten at the water's edge as I moved towards the trail. The creature growled again, a low, rumbling sound that seemed to vibrate right through me.

I turned and bolted, my heart hammering in my chest. The trail was narrow and uneven, the roots and rocks making it difficult to run. I stumbled and nearly fell, but I didn't dare look back. The sound of heavy footsteps followed me, growing louder and more frantic.

The trail seemed to stretch on forever, my lungs burning and my legs aching. I could hear the creature crashing through the underbrush behind me, its heavy breathing filling the air. I pushed myself harder, my fear driving me forward.

Finally, I burst into the clearing where my truck was parked. I fumbled with the keys, my hands shaking, and threw open the door. I scrambled inside, slamming the door shut and locking it. I sat there for a moment, gasping for breath, my heart in my throat.

The creature emerged from the trail, standing at the edge of the clearing. It was even more terrifying up close, its massive form dominating the space. It stared at me through the windshield, its black eyes seemingly staring into my soul. I could see the details of its face now—broad and flat, with a pronounced brow ridge and a wide, almost human-like nose. Its mouth was partially open, revealing sharp, yellowed teeth. It looked almost human yet it also looked like an animal.

Then, with a final huff, the creature turned slowly and walked back into the forest, disappearing into the brush. I sat there, my mind reeling, trying to process what had just happened.

I don't know how long I sat there, but eventually, I managed to pull myself together. I started the truck and drove back to town, my hands gripping the steering wheel like I'd never before.

When I finally reached home, I parked the truck and sat there for a long time, staring at the house. My wife, Emily, was waiting for me on the porch, her expression worried. She knew something was wrong the moment she saw me.

I shook my head, still trying to find the words to explain what I had seen. The fear and disbelief in her eyes mirrored my own.

In the following months, I started fishing again but never at that inlet. I haven't been back since, and I likely never will.

TENNESSEE WILD MAN

TENNESSEE

My name is Rick and I've been huntin' the woods of Tennessee since I was a young boy. There ain't much out there in the forests that can spook me. But one late October day about 10 years ago, I came face to face with somethin' that shook me to my core, somethin' I never thought I'd see in a lifetime of tramping through these woods.

The air was chilly and invigorating when I set out to check my trail cams. I'd been trackin' deer movements for weeks, gettin' ready for the upcoming huntin' season. The trail cams were set deep in the forest, in a spot I'd found a few years back that always seemed to attract the biggest bucks. It was quiet, peaceful, and far from the beaten path. Just how I liked it.

I loaded up my old truck with my gear and my trusty rifle. I wasn't expectin' trouble, but you never know what you might run into out there—coyotes, bears, or the occasional poacher. My dog Buddy, a loyal old mutt, hopped into the passenger seat. He loved the woods as much as I did and was always up for an adventure.

The drive to the trailhead was uneventful. The leaves were turnin', paintin' the forest in shades of red, orange, and yellow. It was the kind of day that made you glad to be alive. I parked the truck, grabbed my gear, and set off down the trail with Buddy at my side.

The hike to the cams was about two miles through dense woods and over some rough terrain. It was a good workout, but I was used to it. The trail cams were spread out over a half-mile area, placed in spots where I'd seen the most deer activity. I figured it would take me a couple of hours to check 'em all and replace the batteries.

The first cam was located near a small clearin'. I approached it quietly, out of habit, even though I wasn't huntin' today. Buddy was sniffin' around, his tail waggin'. I checked the cam, swapped out the SD card, and replaced the batteries. Everythin' looked fine.

As I moved to the second cam, Buddy suddenly stopped and growled low in his throat. I froze, my senses on high alert. Buddy was a good dog, and he didn't growl without a reason. I scanned the trees, lookin' for any sign of movement. The forest was still, the only sound the rustlin' of leaves in the breeze.

"Come on, Buddy," I said softly, tryin' to reassure him. "It's probably just a squirrel."

But Buddy didn't move. He stood there, growlin', his eyes fixed on somethin' in the distance. I followed his gaze, but I couldn't see anythin'. I felt myself suddenly stiffen, and for the first time, I felt uneasy. I shook it off and continued to the next cam, Buddy reluctantly followin'.

The second cam was about a hundred yards away, near a thick stand of pines. I was swappin' out the batteries when I heard it—a gravelly, ominous growl, deeper and more menacing than anythin' I'd ever heard before. It seemed to come from everywhere and nowhere all at once. Buddy went rigid, his hackles raised.

I stood up slowly, my heart poundin' in my chest. The growl came again, louder this time, and I felt the ground vibrate beneath my feet. I clutched my rifle, my knuckles white, and scanned the trees. Just then I saw it—a massive, hulking figure movin' through the woods, just at the edge of my vision.

It was at least seven feet tall, dark hair covering its whole body. Its shoulders were broad—I'd guess at least 4 feet wide. The creature moved in a deliberate, almost lazy way, like it had all the time in the world. I was tryin' to make sense of what I was seein'.

"Tennessee Wild Man," I whispered to myself, the

words soundin' absurd even as I said them. But there it was, as real as the rifle in my hands.

I backed away slowly, my eyes never leavin' the creature. It stopped and looked at me, its eyes dark and evil looking. The air around me seemed to grow colder, and I could see my breath in the air. I was terrified, every instinct screamin' at me to run, but I couldn't move.

The creature let out another growl, a sound that seemed to reverberate through my very bones. Buddy whimpered and pressed against my leg. I took a step back, then another, tryin' to put some distance between us. The creature watched me, its eyes unblinkin', its expression unreadable.

I turned and ran, my heart poundin' in my ears. Buddy was right beside me, his ears flat against his head. I didn't look back, didn't dare to. The forest was a blur as I sprinted down the trail. I could hear the creature crashin' through the underbrush next to me, its footsteps heavy and relentless.

I reached the third cam, but I didn't stop. I sprinted past it, headin' for the truck as fast as my tired legs could carry me. The noise of the creature grew fainter, but I didn't slow down. I didn't feel safe until I was back in the clearin', the truck in sight.

I threw my gear into the back and climbed into the driver's seat, slammin' the door shut. Buddy jumped in beside me, his eyes wide with fear. I started the engine and peeled out of there, gravel flyin' as I sped down the road. I wasn't hangin' around for nobody!

I don't remember much of the drive back to town. I'd heard stories of the Tennessee Wild Man, or what others call Bigfoot, but I'd never believed 'em. Had never even considered it, really.

I couldn't bring myself to go back to the woods for weeks. When I finally did, I was on edge the entire time, my senses heightened, my rifle always within reach. I checked the trail cams, but there was nothin' unusual on the footage. No sign of the creature, no explanation for what I'd seen.

I used to feel at home in the woods, but now, I felt like an intruder.

I started carryin' my rifle everywhere, even when I wasn't huntin'. I didn't go out alone, always bringin' Buddy or a friend.

THE HAUNTING OF ROSEWOOD FARM

OKLAHOMA

When you grow up on a pig farm in Oklahoma, you learn to respect the land and the creatures that inhabit it. Life on the farm teaches you about hard work, responsibility, and sometimes, fear.

My name is Lila, and I'm forty years old now. Looking back on my childhood, there's one series of encounters that triggered my anxiety issues and have haunted me ever since. It happened when I was just a girl living on Rosewood Farm, our family property.

I was about ten years old when the strange occurrences began. Rosewood Farm was an expansive ranch with gently sloping meadows, thick forests, and a creek that meandered through the property. We raised pigs, and my parents worked tirelessly to keep the farm running smoothly. My brother, Ethan, and I helped out where we could, feeding the pigs, cleaning the pens, and doing other chores.

It was late summer, and the days were long and hot. The air was thick with the smell of hay, mud, and the earthy scent of the pigs. One evening, just as the sun was setting, I was out in the yard playing with our dog, Daisy. She was a lively border collie, always full of energy and eager to chase anything that moved.

I was tossing a stick for Daisy when she suddenly stopped, her ears perked up and her body tense. She stared at the edge of the woods, a low growl rumbling in her throat. I followed her gaze, but all I could see were the shadows of the trees.

"Daisy, come on," I called, but she didn't move. She just kept growling, her eyes fixed on something I couldn't see.

I suddenly felt very uneasy. The woods had always been a place of adventure and wonder for me, but in that moment, they seemed dark and foreboding. I grabbed Daisy's collar and led her back to the house, anxiety growing in my chest.

That night, as I lay in bed, I couldn't shake the feeling of unease. The image of Daisy growling at the woods replayed in my mind, and I found myself straining to hear any unusual sounds. The farm was quiet, save for the occasional grunt from the pigs and the wind through the trees.

Over the next few days, strange things started happening around the farm. We found the remains of a few pigs, their bodies mutilated in ways that no predator we knew could manage. My parents were baffled and concerned. They set up traps and reinforced the pens, but the attacks continued.

One evening, just before dusk, my father and Ethan went out to check the traps. I stayed behind with my mother, helping her prepare dinner. Daisy was restless, pacing back and forth and growling at the slightest noise. Suddenly, she bolted out the door, barking furiously.

"Daisy, come back!" I shouted, but she was already halfway to the woods.

I grabbed a flashlight and ran after her, my mother calling out for me to be careful. The light from the setting sun cast long shadows across the yard, making everything seem creepy and distorted. I followed Daisy's barking, the flashlight beam bouncing wildly as I ran.

I reached the edge of the woods and stopped, my breath coming in ragged gasps. Daisy was standing a few yards ahead, barking at something in the darkness. I shone the flashlight in her direction and froze.

Standing just beyond the reach of the light was a massive human-shaped figure. The only features I could see clearly were its red eyes. They were glowing and the sheer size of this thing absolutely petrified me. The creature just stood there, slightly swaying, but its presence filled me with a sense of dread I had never felt before.

I wanted to scream, to run, but I couldn't move. My feet felt like they were rooted to the ground, and my voice seemed to be stuck in my throat. Daisy continued to bark, her fur bristling, but the creature didn't move. It just stood there, staring at us.

I have no idea how long I was standing there but I suddenly felt a wave of nausea take over me. Daisy whimpered and backed away, her tail between her legs. I finally found my voice and screamed, the sound echoing through the trees.

The creature turned and melted into the woods like it was never there. I grabbed Daisy and ran back to the house, tears streaming down my face. My mother was waiting on the porch, her face etched with worry.

"What happened?" she asked, pulling me into her arms.

I could barely speak, my words coming out in a jumbled mess. "There was something... in the woods... it was huge."

My mother held me tight, her expression serious. "We'll tell your father when he gets back. For now, let's get inside."

That night, I couldn't sleep. Every time I closed my eyes, I saw the creature's glowing red eyes staring at me. I tossed and turned and pictured the creature bursting through the front door and coming for me.

The next morning, I told my father and Ethan what had happened. They listened intently, their faces growing more serious with every word. My father decided to set up more traps and reinforce the fences even further. He also gave me strict instructions not to go near the woods or let Daisy out alone.

Life on the farm continued, but things were never the same. The attacks on the pigs continued sporadically, each one more brutal than the last. My father stayed up late at night, keeping watch with his rifle, but he never saw the creature.

One night, about a week after my encounter, I was awakened by a strange noise. It was a low, rumbling growl, almost like the one I'd heard before, but this time it was closer. I sat up in bed, my heart pounding, and listened.

The growl came again, followed by the sound of something heavy moving outside my window. I climbed out of bed and crept to the window, peeking out through the curtains. The moon was full, casting a pale light over the yard.

I saw it again—the massive figure, standing near the pig pen. It was bent over, its large hands gripping the wooden fence. It looked up, and for a moment, our eyes met. I felt a wave of terror wash over me, my breath catching in my throat.

The creature huffed and turned its attention back to

the pen. It grabbed one of the pigs, lifting it effortlessly and snapping its neck with a sickening crack. I wanted to scream, to wake my parents, but I was paralyzed with fear.

The creature stood up, holding the lifeless pig in its hands. It looked around, its eyes glowing in the moonlight, before turning and disappearing into the woods. I backed away from the window, my whole body trembling.

I didn't sleep for the rest of the night. When morning came, I told my parents what I had seen. My father went out to the pen, his face grim. The pig was gone, and the fence was damaged. He decided it was time to call in help.

We contacted the local authorities, but they were skeptical. They sent someone out to take a look, but there wasn't much they could do. They suggested it might be a bear, but I knew better. Bears didn't have glowing red eyes and walk on two feet!

The encounters continued, each one worse than the last. The creature seemed to be toying with us, always staying just out of reach. I started to dread the nights, knowing that it was out there, somewhere.

One evening, as the sun was setting, I was out feeding the pigs. My father was in the barn, fixing a broken gate, and my mother was inside cooking dinner. Daisy was by my side, her ears perked up and her nose twitching.

Suddenly, she started growling, her eyes fixed on the edge of the woods. I felt my legs go weak and turned to look.

There it was again, the massive figure standing in the shadows, watching me.

I backed away slowly, my heart pounding. Daisy barked furiously, but the creature didn't move. It just stood there, its red eyes glowing. I wanted to run, but I knew I had to stay calm.

I called out for my father, my voice shaking. "Dad! It's here!"

He came running out of the barn, his rifle in hand. He saw the creature and stopped in his tracks, his eyes wide with shock. The creature growled and took a step forward, and my father raised his rifle.

"Get inside, Lila!" he shouted, his voice filled with urgency.

I grabbed Daisy and ran to the house, my legs feeling like they were made of lead. My mother was waiting on the porch, calling my name. She pulled me inside and locked the door.

We heard a gunshot, followed by a loud, angry roar. My mother held me tight, her hands trembling. I wanted to go back out, to help my father, but she wouldn't let me.

The roaring continued, followed by more gunshots. Then, everything went silent. My mother and I waited, our hearts pounding, until finally, we heard my father's voice.

"It's gone," he said, his voice tired and strained. "For

now."

We stayed inside for the rest of the night, my father keeping watch with his rifle. The next morning, we found the tracks—huge, deep prints in the mud leading into the forest with blood drops here and there.

The encounters stopped after that night, but the anxiety never left me. I knew that monsters existed now and it was every child's worse nightmare come to life.

As I grew older, I moved away from the farm, went to college, and started a family of my own.

Now, at forty years old, I still think about those nights on Rosewood Farm. The fear that creature instilled in me was something I will never get over. I have never told anyone of our experiences, not even my husband and I doubt I ever will.

THE BEAST OF BLACKWATER FARM

There's a sense of pride that comes from living off the land, especially here in Alabama. Earl is my name and I've been farming Blackwater Farm since my daddy passed it down to me, just like his daddy did before him. There's not much that can shake a man who's weathered storms, droughts, and the relentless toil of the earth. But there's one encounter, one memory that still makes me shiver no matter how many times I try to forget it.

It was a sweltering August night, one of those where the air is so thick you can practically chew it. The cicadas were singing their nightly chorus, and the frogs by the pond were croaking loud enough to wake the dead. My wife, Betsy, was in the kitchen canning tomatoes, and I was out on the porch, sipping a cold beer and enjoying the brief respite from the day's work. Our old coonhound, Duke, lay sprawled at my feet, twitching every now and then in his sleep.

I reckon it was close to midnight when I first noticed something was off. Duke suddenly lifted his head, his ears perked up, and he let out a low, menacing growl. Now, Duke's a good dog—loyal, protective, but not one to get riled up without a good reason. I followed his gaze out towards the edge of the woods, but all I could see were shadows.

"Easy, boy," I muttered, giving him a reassuring pat. But he didn't settle. Instead, he stood up, his growl growing louder, more insistent.

I grabbed my flashlight and rifle, just in case. You never know what kind of critters might wander onto the farm, especially at night. "Betsy, I'm gonna go check on something," I called out, though I doubt she heard me over the racket in the kitchen.

I stepped off the porch, Duke by my side, and made my way towards the tree line. The beam of my flashlight cut through the darkness, but all it showed were the familiar shapes of trees and underbrush. Still, it felt like something was out there with us.

As we approached the woods, Duke suddenly took off, barking like a madman. I hurried after him, my heart leaping in my chest. "Duke! Get back here!" I hollered, but he was already out of sight.

I plunged into the woods, the flashlight beam bouncing wildly as I ran. The cicadas and frogs had fallen eerily silent, and the only sound was my heavy breathing and the crunch of leaves under my boots.

That's when I nearly ran into it—an unbelievably large beast, standing right there in the beam of my flashlight. I stumbled back as I realized what I was seeing. I could see how thick its legs were, how long its arms were, and the sinister look on its ugly face. It must've been at least nine feet tall, maybe more. My breath caught in my throat when I saw its red eyes, and I felt a cold sweat break out on my forehead.

"Duke, get back here!" I called again, my voice trembling. The beast didn't move, didn't even flinch. It just stood there, staring at me intently with eyes that seemed to glow a deep, evil red.

I raised my rifle, my hands shaking, and took a step back. "Get outta here!" I demanded, trying to sound braver than I felt. The beast remained silent, its gaze never leaving mine.

Then, with a lowest growl I have ever heard, it looked at my rifle and then back at me. Did it recognize what a gun was and what damage it could do? This was no dumb animal. It was damn intelligent and I have never felt so vulnerable in my life.

"Stay back!" I shouted, but the beast stood its ground. I fired a shot into the air, the sound echoing through the trees. The beast stopped, its growl turning into a snarl. For a moment, I thought it was going to rush me, the tension thick enough to cut with a knife.

Then, after glancing down at Duke, I looked back up and it was gone. Just like that. I stood there, baffled yet relieved.

Duke came trotting back, his tail between his legs. He looked up at me, and whimpered. "Come on, boy," I said, my voice shaking. "Let's get back to the house."

We made our way back to the farm, my mind mush. What had I just encountered? A booger? A Sasquatch? I'd seen the movies and heard the tales but I'd never seen anything so strange in all my years on the farm. I guess, until now.

When I got back to the house, Betsy was waiting on the porch, a worried look on her face. "What happened, Earl? You look like you've seen a ghost."

I shook my head, trying to find the words. "I don't know, Betsy. I think…I think I saw something out there. Some sort of beast."

She frowned, her concern deepening. "What do you mean, a beast?"

"I don't know. It wasn't a bear, or any animal I've ever

seen. It was…it was like a man, but bigger. Hairier."

Betsy's eyes widened. "You mean like a booger?"

I nodded slowly. "Yeah, maybe. I don't know what else it could've been."

That night, I couldn't sleep. Every time I closed my eyes, I saw those glowing red eyes staring back at me. The farm felt different, less safe. I kept my rifle close, listening for any sound that might signal the creature's return. I was constantly on edge.

The next day, I went out to the woods with a couple of friends, hoping to find some sign of the creature. We searched for hours, but found nothing—no tracks, no broken branches, no evidence that anything unusual had been there. It was like the creature had vanished without a trace.

Now years later, I never saw the beast again and boy, am I glad about that. I have grandchildren now and when they are playing in the yard, I still keep a watchful eye on them just in case it decides to turn up again.

THE FACE IN THE BUSHES

NORTH CAROLINA

I'm a simple man. My name's Roger and I was born and raised on a small farm in North Carolina. I've spent my whole life working this land, growing crops, tending to animals, and living a quiet, uncomplicated life. The farm's been in my family for generations, and I've always found a sense of peace and purpose in its daily rhythms. But there's one memory, one encounter that still haunts me to this day, something I never thought I'd experience in a lifetime of farming.

It was a late afternoon in mid-September, the kind of day where the air is clean and the leaves are just starting to turn. The sun was sinking low in the sky, casting shadows across the fields. I was finishing up my chores, making sure everything was in order before heading inside for supper.

My dog, Rusty, a fun-loving old golden retriever, was sniffing around the yard, his nose to the ground as usual.

As I was putting away some tools in the barn, I heard movement in the brush near the edge of the field. At first, I thought it was just the wind stirring the leaves, but then Rusty started barking, his ears perked up and his tail stiff. That dog had a nose for trouble, and when he got riled up, I knew it was worth checking out.

I grabbed my flashlight and headed towards the sound, Rusty at my heels. The rustling grew louder as I approached a thick patch of bushes near the old oak tree. The light was fading fast, and the shadows were growing deeper, making everything look more sinister than usual.

"Rusty, hush now," I muttered, trying to calm him down. He kept barking, though, his eyes fixed on the bushes.

I shone my flashlight into the underbrush, but at first, I didn't see anything unusual. The beam of light cut through the darkness, illuminating the dense foliage. I took a few steps closer, my heart starting to beat a little faster. Rusty growled low in his throat, and I could feel the hairs on the back of my neck standing up.

"Hello?" I called out, my voice sounding shaky even to my own ears. "Anyone there?"

No answer, just more rustling. I edged closer, my flashlight trembling in my hand. That's when I saw it—a pair of eyes, glowing a dull red in the darkness. They were set deep in a face and wide apart. The creature was crouched low, partially hidden by the bushes, but I could make out enough to know that it wasn't any animal I was familiar with.

The face was broad and covered in coarse, thick hair. Its nose was flat, somewhat like a humans, and its mouth was set in a deep scowl, revealing sharp, yellowed teeth. The eyes, though—they were the worst part. They stared at me with an intensity that made my blood run cold, filled with a mix of curiosity and malice.

I stood there, gob-smacked at what I was seeing. The creature growled, the sound vibrating through my guts. Rusty barked furiously, but I couldn't tear my eyes away from that sinister face. It's face looked so evil.

Without warning, the creature lunged forward, its scowling face coming closer. I stumbled backward, near-ly dropping my flashlight. Fear surged through me, and I turned and ran, Rusty right behind me. My heart pounded in my chest, and I was gasping for breath. I didn't look back, didn't dare to. I just ran as fast as I could, hoping Rusty and I could make it to the front door.

I burst into the house, slamming the door behind me. My wife, Diana, looked up from the kitchen, startled by my sudden entrance.

"Roger, what on earth's the matter?" she asked, her eyes wide with concern.

I leaned against the door, trying to catch my breath. "There's… there's something out there," I managed to say, my voice trembling. "Something in the bushes."

Diana frowned, setting down the dish she was holding. "What do you mean, something?"

"I don't know," I replied, shaking my head. "It was big, and it had a face… a horrible face. A face you'd never want to see, Diana."

She walked over to me, placing a hand on my arm. "Are you sure, hon? Maybe it was just a trick of the light, or just an animal you've never seen before."

I shook my head again, more vigorously this time. "No, Diana. I know what I saw. It wasn't any animal. It was something else. Something menacing."

We spent the rest of the evening locked inside the house, the doors and windows securely shut. I kept my rifle close, just in case as I sat at the kitchen table just staring at the front door, hoping this thing wasn't brave enough to come in the house.

The next morning, I decided to go back to the bushes and see if I could find any evidence of the creature. Diana was worried, but I reassured her that I'd be careful. Rusty was reluctant to follow me, but with a bit of coaxing, he eventually came along.

The sunlight made everything seem less frightening,

but I was still on edge as I approached the spot where I'd seen the creature. I examined the ground carefully, looking for tracks or any other signs that might explain what I'd seen.

Sure enough, I found something—large footprints. They were too big to be a bear, and the shape was all wrong. The prints were deep, indicating something heavy had passed through. I followed them for a short distance, but they disappeared into the thicker underbrush. I wasn't about to go into the woods and look for this darn thing.

Over the next few days, every time I went outside, I found myself glancing towards the bushes, half-expecting to see those glowing eyes staring back at me. Rusty seemed on edge too, his ears constantly perked up, and his eyes always scanning the tree line.

Eventually, life continued on. Rusty went back to being his happy self and I tried putting that evil face out of my head. I always remained cautious though, much more than I had ever been.

THE AIRBNB ENCOUNTER

ARIZONA

I've always been a skeptic. Ghosts, UFOs, Bigfoot—I have really thought about that stuff. I grew up in California, surrounded by the rationality and skepticism that comes with city life. I preferred the concrete certainty of urban existence to the wild speculation of the unknown. That is until a trip to Arizona changed everything I thought I knew.

My name is Jessica, and this is the story of how I became a believer.

I had traveled to Arizona to visit my aunt and uncle, who live in a small town near Flagstaff. I decided to stay in a quiet Airbnb not far from their house. It was a charming little place, tucked away in the woods with a picturesque view of the mountains. The idea was to enjoy some solitude and relaxation after a stressful few months at work in San Francisco.

The first couple of days were blissful. I spent my mornings hiking the nearby trails and my afternoons lounging on the patio with a good book. The air was clean, a welcome change from the smog of the city. I felt at peace, surrounded by nature, with nothing but the sounds of birds and small critters running around to keep me company.

On the third day, I decided to take a longer hike. There was a trail that wound up the mountain and promised stunning views at the top. I packed a small lunch, grabbed my water bottle, and set off early in the morning. The hike was invigorating, the trail well-marked and easy to follow. I felt a sense of freedom and exhilaration as I climbed higher and higher, leaving the world behind.

About halfway up the mountain, I started to feel uneasy. It was subtle at first, just a tingling sensation at the back of my neck. I brushed it off as paranoia, telling myself it was just the isolation playing tricks on my mind. But the feeling persisted, growing stronger with each step. I glanced around, scanning the trees for any sign of movement, but saw nothing.

I tried to shake it off, focusing on the beauty of the scenery and the challenge of the climb. But as I reached the summit, the unease turned into a sense of dread. It felt like I was being watched, like something was out there, just beyond my line of sight. I stood at the top, taking in the breathtaking view, but my mind was elsewhere, consumed by the feeling of being observed.

I decided to cut my hike short and head back down, worried it was a mountain lion or some crazy vagrant. The descent was quicker, but the sense that someone, or something, was following me, never left. Rustling sounds in the underbrush made my heart race, and every snap of a twig had me spinning around, expecting to see something—or someone—hiding in the shadows. But the trail remained empty, the woods silent.

When I finally reached the Airbnb, I felt a wave of relief. I locked the door behind me, feeling safe within the walls of the little house. I laughed at myself, thinking how silly I had been, letting my imagination run wild. I spent the rest of the day trying to relax, and putting the strange feeling out of my mind.

That night, I tossed and turned, unable to sleep. Around midnight, I heard a noise outside—a soft thump, followed by a rustling sound. My heart leapt into my throat. I listened, straining to hear over the pounding of my own heartbeat.

The noise came again, this time closer. I sat up in bed, my eyes wide in the darkness. I was trying to come up with a rational explanation. A deer, maybe, or a raccoon. What other animals lived in the desert? Then I realized it wasn't on four legs. It sounded bipedal and I thought back to it being some crazy vagrant.

I got out of bed and crept to the window. I peeked

through the curtains, my breath catching in my throat. The moonlight cast eerie shadows across the yard, but I couldn't see anything out of the ordinary. Just trees and shrubs, the same as always.

I was about to turn away when something moved at the edge of the forest. I froze, my eyes locked on the spot. A tall, dark figure emerged from the shadows, moving slowly. My heart pounded as I tried to process what I was seeing.

The figure was massive, maybe 7-9 feet tall. Like a linebacker in width. It was covered in dark hair, except for its face and as it stepped into the moonlight, I could see its face clearly—flat and wide, with deep-set eyes that seemed to glow with an inner light. The stuff nightmares are made of.

I gasped, stumbling backward, my mind reeling. This couldn't be real. Bigfoot? In Arizona? I had always dismissed the stories as nonsense, but here it was, standing in front of me. The creature turned its head, and I felt its gaze lock onto me. Goosebumps spread all over my body, and I felt an overwhelming sense of fear. I thought I was going to be sick.

The creature just stood there, its eyes never seeming to leave me. I backed away from the window, my hands shaking. I didn't know what to do. My mind raced with panic. Should I call the police? My aunt and uncle? But what would I say? That I saw a Bigfoot?

I decided to stay put and hope that the creature would

go away. I crept back to bed, pulling the covers up to my chin like a frightened child. I lay there, listening to the sounds outside, my heart pounding in my ears. The rustling grew louder, closer. I heard a soft thump, then another, and then silence. I started praying over and over hoping whatever it was would just go away.

I waited, holding my breath, my body tense with fear. Minutes passed, then an hour, and still, I heard nothing. I finally drifted off to a restless sleep, my dreams filled with images of glowing eyes and dark figures.

The next morning, I awoke with my mind instantly flashing back to the previous night's events. The sun was shining, casting a warm glow across the room. I lay there for a moment, trying to shake off the lingering sense of dread. Had it all been a dream? A product of my overactive imagination?

I got up and dressed, feeling a little better in the daylight. But as I stepped outside to get some fresh air, I noticed something that freaked me the hell out. The ground near the edge of the forest was disturbed, as if something heavy had walked there. Large, deep footprints led from the woods to the house, then back again.

I stared at the prints in disbelief. It hadn't been a dream. The creature had been real, and it had come closer than I had realized. I felt a wave of panic. I couldn't stay here, not with that thing out there.

I packed my bags in a hurry, my hands shaking as I

threw my belongings into my suitcase. I didn't care about getting my money back; I just wanted to get out of there. I called my aunt and uncle, telling them I had to leave early due to an emergency. They sounded concerned, but I didn't give them any details. I didn't want them to think I was crazy.

As I drove away from the Airbnb, I glanced back at the house one last time. It looked peaceful, idyllic even, but I knew better. The creature was real. I vowed never to return.

The drive back to California was long and exhausting.

When I finally reached home, I felt a sense of relief. The familiar sights and sounds of the city brought me comfort, but the memory of that night in Arizona never left me. I will never stay somewhere in the woods or away from civilization again. I would never be able to relax, wondering if there was another creature nearby.

LOGIC CAN'T EXPLAIN THIS

I've always considered myself a rational person. I'm a math teacher, for heaven's sake. Numbers, logic, and reason have been my companions throughout my life. Ghost stories and cryptid tales have always seemed like the stuff of overactive imaginations. Then, one cold autumn morning in Michigan, something happened that shattered my skepticism forever.

My name is Sascha, and this is the story of the morning that changed everything for me.

It was a typical Tuesday morning in the last days of October, and the air was brisk with the promise of winter. I'd woken up early, as usual, to get ready for work. The sun was just beginning to rise, casting a pale, orange glow over the horizon. I grabbed a thermos of coffee, kissed my husband and cat Bella goodbye, and headed out the door.

My commute to the high school where I teach was about twenty minutes, mostly along rural roads that cut through dense forests and fields. It was a peaceful drive, one I'd always enjoyed for its serenity. The leaves were in full color, a riot of reds, oranges, and yellows that made the landscape look like it was on fire. It beat spending an hour in city traffic every day!

I was about ten minutes into my drive, cruising along at a steady pace, when I first noticed something strange. The road ahead seemed darker, like a shadow had fallen across it. I slowed down, squinting to see through the dim light of dawn.

Then I saw what I thought was a bear—an enormous, dark silhouette moving across the road. But as I got closer, I realized it was walking on two legs. I felt my stomach lurch as I squinted into the light, my mind not comprehending what I was seeing.

The figure stepped into the middle of the road, and I slammed on the brakes, my car skidding to a stop just a few yards away. The creature turned to face me, and I felt terror grip me.

It wasn't a bear. It was a man—or at least, it had the shape of a man. But it was massive, probably eight feet tall, with a build like Arnold Schwarzenegger. Its body was covered in thick, auburn hair, and its face… its face was like something out of a nightmare.

The creature's eyes locked onto mine, and I felt paralyzed. Its gaze was intense, almost intelligent, and filled with a strange mix of curiosity and menace. Its nose was flat and wide, and its lips were thin and its mouth extremely wide. I could see its teeth—like ours but so much bigger—and its breath misted in the cold morning air.

Then, as suddenly as it had appeared, the creature turned its head and looked into the forest. It then walked to the side of the road and stopped at the edge of the trees and looked back at me, its eyes glinting in the dim light. I could see the muscles rippling beneath its hair. For a moment, I thought it was going to come back, but it simply stood there, watching me.

I took a deep breath, trying to choose what to do next. I slowly eased my foot off the brake and pressed down on the gas pedal. The car started to move, and I inched forward, my eyes never leaving the creature.

As I drove past, it followed me with its gaze, turning its head to keep me in sight. My hands were shaking so badly that I could barely keep the car on the road. I kept driving, my eyes flicking between the rear view mirror and the road ahead.

I didn't breathe easy until I was miles away, the creature and the forest far behind me. My heart was still pounding, and my mind was a whirlwind of fear and confusion. What had I just seen? It couldn't have been real. But it was. I knew it was.

When I finally reached the school, I sat in the parking lot for a few minutes, trying to calm down. My hands were still shaking, and I felt like I was in a daze. I took a few deep breaths, trying to steady myself. I had to go on with my day, had to teach my classes, but it felt like my world had been turned upside down.

The day passed in a blur. I went through the motions, teaching my students and grading papers, but my mind was elsewhere. I kept replaying the encounter over and over in my head, trying to make sense of it. But no matter how many times I thought about it, I couldn't come up with a logical explanation.

When I got home that evening, I told my husband, Joseph, about what had happened. He listened patiently, but I don't think he believe me. He tried to reassure me, saying that it was probably just a bear or some other animal. But I knew what I had seen.

I avoided the road where it had happened, taking a longer route to work that added an extra fifteen minutes to my commute. I couldn't bring myself to drive down that road again, not after what I had seen. The fear was too real, too intense.

How could such a creature exist, hidden in the forests of Michigan?

It's been a few years since that morning, but I still think about it from time to time. The fear has lessened, but it's never completely gone away. I've learned to live with it, to accept that there are things in this world that defy explanation.

THE HOWLING NIGHTMARE

ALASKA

I never thought I'd find myself writing about something like this. I'm a pragmatist by nature, a businessman from California, used to the hustle and bustle of city life. My name is Joel, and I've always found comfort in numbers, logic, and predictability. However, during a guided hunting trip in the Alaskan wilderness, an event occurred that shattered my understanding of reality.

It was late September when I decided to take a break from the office and join a group of friends on a hunting trip in Alaska. I'd always been an outdoors-man at heart, and the idea of spending a week in the pristine wilderness, far from the stress of daily life, was too tempting to pass up. My buddies and I had planned the trip for months, and we were all terribly excited as we boarded the small sea plane that would take us deep into the heart of the Alaskan wilderness.

Our guide, Jim, was a seasoned hunter with decades of experience. He knew the land like the back of his hand and assured us that we were in for the adventure of a lifetime. The plane ride was breathtaking, offering stunning views of snow-capped mountains, dense forests, and crystal-clear rivers. We landed on a remote lake, surrounded by nothing but untamed wilderness as far as the eye could see.

The first few days were everything I had hoped for. We hunted during the day, hiking through the rugged terrain, and returned to camp in the evenings to share stories around the fire. The air was so clean, the landscape untouched and wild. It felt like we had stepped back in time to a world where nature reigned supreme.

But on the fourth night, everything changed.

We had just finished dinner and were sitting around the campfire, the flickering flames casting long shadows in the darkness. The sky was clear, the stars shining brightly overhead. It was a perfect night, or so we thought.

It started with a distant howl, a sound that seemed to echo through the trees. At first, we thought it was a wolf, but there was something off about it, something not quite right. The howl was deep and resonant, not something I had ever heard before.

Jim frowned, his eyes scanning the darkness. "That's

not a wolf," he said, his voice low and serious. "I've never heard anything like that out here."

We sat in silence, listening as the howling continued, growing louder and more insistent. Then, from the opposite direction, came another howl, followed by a series of hoots and whoops. It sounded like there were multiple creatures out there, communicating with each other.

My heart started to race, a sense of unease settling over me. I looked at my friends, and I could see the same fear reflected in their eyes. We were not alone in the woods.

Jim stood up, grabbing his rifle. "Everyone stay close to the fire," he instructed.

We huddled together, our eyes darting around the darkness. The howling and hooting continued, coming from all directions. It felt like we were surrounded, like the creatures were closing in on us. I gripped my rifle tightly, my hands trembling.

The noises grew louder, more frantic. It sounded like a cacophony of voices, some high-pitched and others low and guttural. The forest seemed to come alive with movement, shadows flickering at the edge of the firelight. I could feel my heart pounding in my chest, my breath coming in short, shallow gasps.

Suddenly, there was a loud crash from the trees, followed by a blood-curdling scream. I jumped to my feet, my adrenaline surging. "What the hell was that?" I shouted, my voice cracking with fear.

Jim didn't answer. He was staring into the darkness, his face pale and tense. "Stay calm," he said, his voice steady but strained. "Don't panic."

We backed away from the fire, forming a tight circle with our rifles at the ready. The noises continued, a symphony of howls, hoots, and screams that seemed to come from every direction. I felt a sense of helplessness, like we were being hunted by something we couldn't see.

Then, out of the darkness, the terror began. It started with a few pebbles, small rocks clattering around our camp. But then, larger stones began to fly, crashing into the ground and thudding against the trees around us. We huddled closer to the fire, our fear growing with each impact.

My heart raced, and I scanned the perimeter of our camp, trying to catch sight of whatever was throwing the rocks. Shadows flickered in the firelight, but we couldn't make out anything definitive. The darkness beyond the firelight was impenetrable, hiding whatever was out there and I felt that whatever was out there knew we couldn't see it.

Another stone came hurtling towards us, landing with a heavy thud just inches from the fire, sending a spray of dirt and embers into the air. My hands shook as I clutched my rifle, afraid for my life.

Jim raised his rifle, aiming into the darkness. "Get

back!" he shouted, his voice filled with authority and desperation.

There was no response, no sound except the rustling of leaves in the night breeze and the crackling of the fire. The rock-throwing continued, relentless and unnerving. I could feel the fear radiating from my friends, and I knew we were all thinking the same thing—how were we going to survive this?

Then, all of a sudden the rock-throwing stopped. An eerie silence settled over the camp, thick and oppressive. We stood there, our hearts pounding, our minds reeling from what we had just experienced. The anticipation of another rock coming our way was overwhelming.

Jim lowered his rifle, his face grim. "We need to get out of here," he said, his voice urgent. "Now."

We didn't argue. We quickly packed up our gear, extinguishing the fire and grabbing our packs. The sense of urgency was unmistakable, the need to leave this place immense. We moved quickly, our eyes scanning the darkness for any sign of the creatures.

The walk back to the lake was tense, every snap of twigs setting us on edge. I felt like we were being watched, like the creatures were stalking us from the shadows. My mind raced with fear and confusion, trying to make sense of what we had seen.

When we finally reached the lake, the first light of dawn

was starting to break over the horizon. The sea plane was anchored near the shore, a beacon of safety in the wilderness. We hurried aboard, our hearts pounding with relief.

As the plane took off, I looked back at the forest, my eyes scanning the trees. And there, standing at the edge of the clearing, was a creature. It watched us with glowing eyes, its presence both terrifying and mesmerizing.

The plane climbed higher, and the creature disappeared from view. I sat back in my seat, my mind racing with thoughts and questions. What had we seen? How could something like that exist?

When we landed back in civilization, I felt a sense of relief wash over me. The familiar sights and sounds of the city brought comfort, but the memory of that night in the Alaskan wilderness never left me.

THE FACE AT THE WINDOW

Hi, I'm Amanda. I'm 32 now, but there's this night from a few years back that still haunts me. I hadn't thought much about it until one of my friends suggested something that I still can't quite wrap my head around. Let me tell you about it.

It happened when I was spending the night at my boyfriend's apartment in High River, Alberta. It was a small block of four apartments, and we were on the bottom floor. I remember it was a quiet night, nothing out of the ordinary. We had gone to bed pretty late after watching a movie and having a few drinks.

Sometime in the middle of the night, I woke up needing to pee. You know how it is, half-asleep and just trying to make your way to the bathroom without fully waking up. After that, I went to the kitchen to get a drink of water. I was still groggy, moving on autopilot.

As I was walking back to the bedroom, something caught my eye. I turned and saw something in the front window. At first, I thought it was just the bushes outside the window swaying, but something seemed off. Perplexed, I took a step forward, trying to make out what it was. The more I looked, the more it started to look like a face.

I dipped my head in a confused way, squinting to get a better look, and then it blinked—it was a face. A huge face taking up three-quarters of the windowpane. I hadn't realized how close it was until I saw those eyes—big, black, and staring right at me. The face had a black leathery texture, a flat nose, and scraggly black hair hanging over it.

I was so startled I dropped the glass I was holding. It shattered on the floor, and I ran back into the bedroom, absolutely terrified. I was bawling my eyes out, trying to tell my boyfriend what I saw, but I could barely get the words out.

He woke up, confused and groggy from the sound of the glass smashing. "What's wrong?" he asked, trying to calm me down.

"There's a face in the front window!" I managed to choke out between sobs.

He looked at me like I was crazy but got up and turned

on the outside light anyway. He couldn't see anything out there. He tried to reassure me, saying it was probably just a cat.

"A cat? Sitting on the bushes? Really?" I replied, feeling a mix of frustration and fear. I knew what I saw, and it was no normal animal. That face...was no bear and definitely not human.

He shrugged it off, and eventually, we went back to bed, though I barely slept a wink. My anxiety was through the roof.

For the longest time, I couldn't figure out what it was. I told a few friends about it, and they all had different theories—some said it was a bear, others thought it might be a prank.

Then, one day, a friend of mine suggested something I had never considered. She said it might have been a Sasquatch. At first, I laughed it off, but the more I thought about it, the more it made sense. I started looking into sightings and stories, and the descriptions matched what I saw that night.

I still don't know for sure what it was, but the thought that it could have been a Sasquatch scares the crap out of me. It's something I never expected to encounter, especially in a small apartment in High River.

To this day, I can't look at that window without remembering that night, and I always close the curtains tight before it gets dark.

MONSTER CHASING THE TRACTOR

The consistent routine of farm life has a comforting familiarity. Our days begin at dawn and often stretch into the night, filled with the unending cycle of chores and the rewarding sight of our hard work taking shape.

My name is Linda, and for the last fifteen years, my husband Dave and I have been tending this farm in Missouri. We've faced down storms, endured droughts, and navigated financial struggles, but nothing could have prepared us for the terrifying experience we had one spring day.

It was late April, and the fields were ripe for plowing. Dave had been out since dawn, working the far field with our old tractor, turning the soil in preparation for planting. The morning air was cool, the sun just beginning to warm the earth. I was inside, finishing up the breakfast dishes, when I decided to take a break and enjoy the fresh air on the patio.

Our house sits on a small rise, giving me a good view of the fields and the edge of the forest beyond. I've always loved this spot, watching the seasons change and the wildlife that occasionally wandered out of the trees. But that morning, I saw something I didn't think existed.

As I sipped my coffee, I noticed a large, dark figure moving at the edge of the forest. At first, I thought it was a deer or maybe a bear, but as it stepped out into the open, my heart skipped a beat. This thing was huge. I have never seen something so big in all my life. It was standing at 8-9 feet tall, with a massive, muscular build like a bodybuilder, a tapered waist and a cone-shaped head. There was no distinguishable neck that I could see but I could see the muscles in its legs move as it ran. It moved with a strange, almost graceful gait, and as it got closer, I realized it was on all fours, galloping toward the field where Dave was plowing.

I felt a surge of panic. From my vantage point, I could see that Dave had his back to the creature and was completely unaware of its presence. I grabbed the radio we always kept on the patio for emergencies and called out to him, my voice shaking.

"Dave, there's something coming out of the woods! It's

heading straight for you!"

There was a moment of static, and then his voice crackled back, confused. "What are you talking about, Linda?"

"Just look behind you!" I shouted, my hands trembling.

I watched as Dave turned in his seat, his mouth dropping as he saw the creature. It was now only a few hundred yards away, moving with terrifying speed. Dave floored the tractor, trying to put some distance between him and the creature, but it easily kept pace, running alongside the tractor with an angry, almost menacing look on its face. It would run up to the tractor and slap it then move away and repeat.

I dropped the radio and ran inside, my heart pounding in my chest. I grabbed the shotgun we kept for protection, my hands shaking so badly I could barely load it. I ran back outside, my mind crazy with fear and desperation.

As the tractor approached the house, the creature was still right beside it, snarling and baring its teeth. I took a deep breath, raised the shotgun, and fired a shot above its head. The sound echoed across the field, and for a moment, everything seemed to stand still.

The creature stopped, its eyes locking onto mine. It was close enough now that I could see the details of its face—somewhat human-like but more primitive, with a pronounced brow ridge, deep-set eyes, a flat, wide nose, and a wide, thin mouth. It let out a low huff sound, and it turned and bolted back toward the forest.

Dave brought the tractor to a halt and jumped down, running toward the house. I lowered the shotgun, my hands still trembling, and met him halfway.

"Did you see that thing?" he gasped, his face pale and sweaty.

I nodded, tears of relief and fear streaming down my face. "What was it, Dave? What did we just see?"

He shook his head, his eyes wide with shock. "I don't know, Linda. It looked like a monster."

We stood there for a long moment, holding each other, the fear and adrenaline slowly subsiding. The fields were quiet now, the only sound the distant chirping of birds. It felt surreal, like a nightmare we couldn't wake up from. It was just so shocking.

That night, neither of us could sleep. We sat in the living room, the shotgun resting on the coffee table between us, and tried to make sense of what had happened. We talked about calling the authorities, but what would we say? That we saw a monster on our property? No-one would believe us and I wouldn't blame them. If someone told me that a week ago, I would have laughed.

In the days that followed, every time I stepped outside, I found myself scanning the tree line, half-expecting to see creature running towards me. Dave couldn't shake the fear either. He started carrying a rifle with him whenever he went out to the fields, and we kept the shotgun loaded and close at hand.

One evening, about a week after the encounter, we were sitting on the porch, watching the sunset. The air was warm and still, the sky painted with hues of orange and pink. It should have been a peaceful moment, but the memory of that creature was still fresh in our minds.

"Do you think it will come back?" I asked, my voice barely above a whisper.

Dave was silent for a moment, his eyes fixed on the tree line. "I don't know, Linda. I hope not."

We never did see the creature again, but the fear never entirely went away. We became more cautious, more aware of our surroundings.

As the months passed, the memory of that day began to fade, but it never disappeared completely. Now, I would never go into the woods without being armed. And armed well.

In the end, life goes on. The seasons change, the crops grow, and the rhythm of farm life continues. But we'll never forget what we saw that day, the creature that emerged from the woods and changed our lives forever.

THE LAST JOB OF THE DAY

Hey y'all, name's Samuel, and I've been a mover for most of my life, workin' outta South Carolina. Now, I've seen a lotta strange things in my life, but nothin' like what happened one late afternoon on the outskirts of town. If you got a minute, let me tell you about the day I saw somethin' that still makes my skin crawl.

It was a hot, sticky day in August, and my partner, Tyson, and I were wrappin' up our last job of the day. We were out at this big ol' house at the edge of town, one of those places where the plots of land are huge and the neighbors are far and few between. The sun was hangin' low in the sky, and we were both tired as hell, just ready to finish up and call it a day.

We pulled up the long driveway and started unloadin' the truck. The homeowners were nice folks, older couple, real sweet. They offered us lemonade and even brought out some cookies while we were workin'. Tyson and I were haulin' furniture and boxes, sweatin' like pigs but pushin' through, knowin' a cold beer was waitin' for us once we were done.

We were about halfway through unloadin' when Tyson suddenly hollered, "Samuel, get in the truck! NOW!"

I paused, wonderin' what the hell had gotten into him. Tyson ain't one to scare easy, so I knew somethin' was up. I turned to see what he was lookin' at and my heart skipped a beat. Comin' across the lawn was this creature, looked like a dog but bigger, way bigger. It was movin' fast, real fast, and it had this look in its eyes that nearly made me wet my pants.

I didn't waste no time. Tyson and I bolted for the truck, slammin' the doors shut and lockin' 'em tight. We sat there, breathin' hard, watchin' as this thing got closer. It stopped just shy of the truck, sniffin' around like it was tryin' to figure out what we were.

"Samuel, what the hell is that?" Tyson whispered, his voice shakin'.

"I don't know, man, but it ain't no regular dog, that's for sure," I replied, my hands grippin' the steering wheel so tight I thought I was going to break it.

We sat there, too scared to move, watchin' this creature. It was built like a dog but had these long, gangly legs and a head that didn't quite fit its body. Its fur was mangy, patches missin', and its eyes… they were too smart, too aware, like it knew exactly what it was doin'.

The creature sniffed around the truck for what felt like forever, then it suddenly took off back across the lawn, disappearin' into the woods. Tyson and I stayed put, too scared to get out, even though we couldn't see it anymore.

"What do we do now?" Tyson asked, lookin' at me with wide eyes.

"We wait," I said, though I had no idea how long we'd have to. "Ain't no way I'm gettin' out there with that thing still hangin' around."

After about 15 minutes, we saw the homeowner walkin' down the driveway. She had a puzzled look on her face, probably wonderin' why we were sittin' in the truck instead of finishin' the job. We watched her approach, and as she got closer, we finally felt a bit safer.

Tyson and I exchanged glances, then slowly unlocked the doors and stepped out, keepin' an eye on the tree line.

"What's goin' on, boys?" the homeowner asked, concern in her voice.

"We saw somethin'," I explained, tryin' to keep my voice steady. "Looked like a big dog, but it wasn't right. Came runnin' at us, and we didn't know what to do."

The homeowner's eyes widened a bit, but she didn't say much. Just nodded and told us she hadn't seen anythin' like that around here before. We finished unloadin' the truck as quick as we could, all the while keepin' an eye out for that creature.

Once we were done, we didn't stick around for chit-chat. Tyson and I jumped in the truck and high-tailed it outta there. We were both quiet on the drive back, replaying the encounter over and over again.

I don't know what that thing was, and I don't ever want to see it again. Tyson and I still talk about it sometimes, tryin' to figure out if we imagined the whole thing, but we both know it was real. Whatever it was, it wasn't no regular animal and that is the last time I ever want to see it.

WHISTLES IN THE MARK TWAIN FOREST

Howdy, y'all. The name's Stephen, and I've been living here in this small house at the edge of the Mark Twain National Forest for a good few years now. I'm pushin' fifty, and like most folks, I've seen my fair share of strange things, but nothin' quite like what I'm about to tell ya. Now, I ain't one for tall tales, but this here's as true as the day is long.

It was a warm summer evenin', just as the sun was settin', and I was out in my driveway tinkerin' with my old truck. She's a beauty, a 1965 Ford F-100, and I like to keep her in tip-top shape. The sky was painted all kinds of colors—reds, oranges, and purples. It was one of those picture-perfect Missouri sunsets.

As I was elbow-deep in grease, tryin' to get the carburetor just right, I started hearin' these whistles comin' from the woods. Now, at first, I thought nothin' of it. Figured it was just some birds callin' to each other. But after a while, I noticed it was more than just one whistle. It sounded like a whole bunch of folks whistlin' back and forth to each other, like they were havin' a conversation or somethin'.

I paused, wiped my hands on a rag, and listened real close. Sure enough, there were at least three or four distinct whistles, answerin' each other from different directions in the woods. It struck me as odd, but I shrugged it off, thinkin' it might be some kids playin' around. Went back to work on the truck, but the whistles kept comin'. They weren't random like birds; they had a rhythm, almost like a pattern.

Curiosity got the better of me, and I set down my wrench and walked over to the edge of the woods. The whistles stopped dead in their tracks the moment I got close. Everything went dead quiet. I stood there for a minute, lookin' around, but there wasn't a soul in sight. Just the trees swayin' in the breeze and the last light of day fadin' away.

Thinkin' it was just some kids havin' a laugh, I went back to my truck. A few minutes later, I started hearin' somethin' else—muffled voices, like folks talkin' but not quite loud enough to make out the words. It was comin' from the woods, and it didn't sit right with me. I stood up and strained to listen, but the chatter was too low to understand. It was like a bunch of people whisperin' all at once.

Now, I ain't one to spook easy, but this was startin' to get under my skin. My beagle, Buddy, who's usually runnin' around sniffin' and barkin' at every critter, was nowhere to be seen. He was huddled up on the porch, shakin' like a leaf. I called out to him, but he wouldn't budge. Just stared at the woods with his ears pinned back.

My girlfriend, Sue, had been stayin' over a lot less lately. She always said the place was creepy at night, and I couldn't blame her. She's a city girl, used to streetlights and the hum of traffic, not the pitch-black darkness and strange noises of the forest. Last time she stayed over, she swore she heard footsteps outside the window and decided she'd had enough. She ain't been back since.

Every now and then, this rank smell would waft in through the windows, smellin' like somethin' crawled outta a swamp and died. When it hit, I had to get up and close the windows quick, or the whole house would reek. It didn't happen often, but when it did, it was enough to make your eyes water.

One night, after hearin' the whistles and chatter for the umpteenth time, I decided to stay up and see if I could catch a glimpse of whatever was makin' the noise. I sat on the porch with my shotgun, just in case, and waited. The night was still, too still. No crickets chirpin', no owls hootin', just an eerie silence that made me feel real uneasy.

A couple hours passed, and just as I was about to give up, I heard it. The low murmur of voices, clearer this time but still unintelligible. They seemed to be comin' closer, and my heart started poundin' in my chest. I strained my eyes, tryin' to see through the darkness, but all I could make out were shadows.

Then, outta nowhere, Buddy started growlin', low and mean. I looked down at him, and his fur was standin' on end. He was starin' at the edge of the woods, his eyes wide and fearful. I followed his gaze, but didn't see a darn thing.

I ain't seen anything yet, but the whistles and chatter still happen from time to time. I don't know what's out there in the Mark Twain Forest, and I don't rightly wanna find out. Sue and I don't talk about it much, and Buddy still refuses to go near the woods.

THE SHADOW IN THE SNOW

My name is Ian, and I'm 25 years old. This past winter, my girlfriend Emma and I decided to take a skiing holiday in Jasper, Alberta. We'd both been to the Alps before, but we wanted to try something different, something more remote and wild. Little did we know that our adventure would take a terrifying turn, one that neither of us will ever forget.

We arrived in Jasper on a crisp, clear day in January. The sky was a brilliant blue, and the snow-covered mountains glistened in the sunlight. It was like stepping into a winter wonderland. Emma and I were both excited and a little nervous, but mostly we were eager to hit the slopes.

We checked into our cozy cabin at the lodge, unpacked

our gear, and headed straight for the ski lifts. The air was cold and invigorating, and the scent of pine trees filled the air. It felt good to be away from the hustle and bustle of London, surrounded by the serene beauty of the Canadian Rockies.

The first few days were perfect. We skied to our hearts' content, exploring the various trails and enjoying the breathtaking views. The runs were long and challenging, but we loved every minute of it. The lodge was charming, with a roaring fire in the main hall and hot cocoa always available. In the evenings, we would sit by the fire, talking about the day's adventures and planning our next runs.

On the third day of our trip, we decided to try a new route that we hadn't explored yet. It was a bit off the beaten path, but we were both confident in our skiing abilities. We took the chair lift to the top of the mountain, chatting excitedly about the fresh powder we hoped to find.

As we ascended, the view was spectacular. The landscape stretched out before us, a sea of white punctuated by dark green forests. Emma was taking pictures with her phone, capturing the beauty of the moment. I was looking forward to the run, anticipating the thrill of carving through untouched snow.

But as we neared the top, something caught my eye. In the distance, near the edge of the forest, I saw a large, dark figure moving through the snow. At first, I thought it was a bear, but as I looked closer, I realized it was walking on two legs. I felt a little excited but at the same time, something just felt off.

I pointed towards the figure, my heart beginning to race. Emma squinted in the direction I was pointing, her expression turning to one of confusion.

The figure was moving steadily through the snow, its long arms swinging at its sides. It was massive, about nine feet tall I would guess, and covered in dark hair. The sight of it sent a shiver down my spine. No human could walk through the snow that fast.

The chair lift continued its ascent, and we lost sight of the figure as we reached the top. Emma and I exchanged worried glances, both of us feeling a sense of unease. I couldn't shake the image of that dark figure from my mind. The forest seemed to loom closer, the shadows darker and more menacing.

We decided to stick to our plan and ski down the new route, but the excitement had been replaced by a sense of trepidation. As we started our descent, I kept looking back towards the forest, expecting to see the figure again. The run was more challenging than we had anticipated. The snow was deeper, and the terrain was rougher. We were both skilled skiers, but the conditions were taxing. My thoughts kept drifting back to the figure we had seen, and I found it hard to focus.

About halfway down the mountain, we stopped to catch our breath. The forest was close now, the trees tall and silent. The air was still, and the only sound was the crunch of our skis on the snow.

Emma and I exchanged a few words, our voices barely above a whisper. The unease was evident, and we both felt it. We decided to keep moving, hoping to shake off the fear that was beginning to take hold. But as we neared the bottom of the run, I felt an overwhelming sense of dread. It was as if we were being watched, the hairs on the back of my neck standing on end.

As we reached the bottom, we saw a group of skiers ahead of us, and the sight brought a wave of relief. We joined them, exchanging pleasantries and trying to act normal. But the encounter had left its mark, and I couldn't shake the feeling that something was out there, waiting to pounce.

That evening, we returned to the lodge, both of us shaken and exhausted. We tried to enjoy dinner and the warmth of the fire, but the image of that dark figure haunted us. We talked about it, confused about what we had seen, but there were no answers.

The next day, we decided to stick to the more populated runs, hoping to avoid any further encounters. But the sense of unease remained. Every shadow seemed to hold a threat, every rustle in the trees a potential danger.

On our last day in Jasper, we decided to take one final run before heading back to the lodge to pack. We chose a familiar route, one that we had skied several times before.

The sky was overcast, and the air was heavy with the promise of snow.

As we ascended the chair lift, I couldn't help but scan the forest below, looking for any sign of the figure. Emma was silent, lost in her thoughts.

We reached the top and started our descent, the snow falling softly around us. The run was smooth, and for a moment, I felt a sense of peace. But as we rounded a bend, a chilling howl echoed through the air.

I skidded to a stop, grabbing Emma's arm. We both stood still, our eyes wide with fear, listening intently. The howl was incredibly loud—deep, resonant, and filled with an unsettling intensity.

My heart leapt into my throat, and a surge of fear gripped me. The sound seemed to come from the edge of the forest, hidden just out of sight. We stood there, paralyzed, trying to compute what we were hearing.

Then, without warning, the howl came again, even closer this time. It reverberated through the trees, sending terror right through us. I could see the fear in Emma's eyes, and I knew we had to get out of there.

We turned and skied as fast as we could, our fear propelling us down the mountain. I could hear my own breath, heavy and labored, my heart pounding in my chest. The eerie howl continued to echo through the forest, driving us into a panic.

When we reached the bottom, we didn't stop. We skied straight to the lodge, our thoughts tangled in anxiety. We burst into the lobby, breathless and wide-eyed, and quickly told the staff about what we had seen.

To our surprise, they took us seriously. One of the staff members, a seasoned local, nodded thoughtfully. "You're not the first to see something like that," he said. "There have been sightings in these parts for years. We call it the Wild Man of the Woods."

We packed our bags and checked out of the lodge, eager to leave Jasper behind. The drive to the airport was tense, both of us lost in our thoughts. The encounter had shaken us to our core, and we couldn't wait to be back in the familiar surroundings of home.

When we finally boarded the plane, I felt I could finally breathe. The thought of leaving the wilderness behind was comforting, but the memory of that dark figure stayed. As the plane took off, I looked out the window at the vast expanse of the Rockies, knowing that somewhere out there, the creature was still roaming.

I've also come to see our experience as a bonding moment for Emma and me. We've faced something terrifying together, and it's strengthened our relationship.

THE WOLF THAT STOOD

MICHIGAN

Nights in Michigan can be long and lonely, especially when you're driving home after a late shift. I've been a nurse for almost twenty years now, and I've seen my fair share of weird things within the hospital walls. Nothing, and I mean nothing, beats the encounter I am about to tell you about that happened on a cold autumn night, driving home from the hospital. My name is Karen, and I'm still trying to make sense of what happened.

It was a Friday night about sixteen years ago, and I'd just finished a twelve-hour shift at St. John's Hospital in Ann Arbor. I was exhausted, my feet aching and my mind numb from the day's work. The drive to my house was usually a peaceful time for me to unwind, to let the events of the day fade away as I made my way through the quiet, dark roads of Michigan.

I live alone, in a small house a few miles outside of Dexter. It's a peaceful place, surrounded by trees and open fields. I've always enjoyed the solitude, the feeling of being close to nature. But that night, the darkness felt different, heavier somehow.

It was around 11 PM when I left the hospital. The roads were empty, and the only light came from the occasional streetlamp and the glow of my car's headlights. I was about halfway home, driving down a stretch of rural road that cuts through dense woods, when I saw something that made scared me beyond belief.

On the side of the road, just at the edge of my headlights, was what looked like a very large wolf. At first, I thought my tired eyes were playing tricks on me. But as I got closer, I realized it was real. It was huge, much larger than any wolf I'd ever seen. Its fur was dark and patchy, and it was crouched low to the ground, as if it were stalking something.

I slowed down, my heart doing back-flips in my chest. The creature's eyes caught the light from my headlights, and they glowed an eerie yellow. Goosebumps suddenly prickled my skin. It didn't move, just stared at me as I approached.

I told myself to keep driving, to get past it as quickly as possible. But as I drew closer, the creature did something that made my heart stop. It stood up.

It stood up on two legs!

I gasped, my hands tightening on the steering wheel. The creature was massive, towering over my car. It looked more like a werewolf from a horror movie than any animal I'd ever seen. Its eyes were locked onto mine, and I could see the muscles rippling under its fur.

Panic took over. I slammed my foot on the gas, speeding past the creature. For a moment, I was sure it was going to lunge at my car, but it just stood there, watching me with those glowing eyes. My heart was racing, and I could barely breathe.

I didn't slow down. I didn't look back. I just kept driving, my mind racing with fear and confusion. I knew I couldn't go home, not with that thing out there. I was terrified it would follow me, that it would find me.

My sister, Nancy, lives about ten miles from my place, closer to town. Without thinking, I changed direction and headed for her house. The drive felt longer than usual, my mind replaying the encounter over and over. What had I seen? How could something like that exist?

When I finally reached Nancy's house, I practically jumped out of the car, my hands shaking as I closed the door. I rang the doorbell repeatedly, my heart pounding in my chest. It took a few moments for Nancy to answer, her face filled with concern when she saw me.

I could barely get the words out. There was something

out there, huge and standing on two legs. She let me in, and I quickly explained what had happened. She listened, her eyes wide with shock. Nancy has always been the more skeptical one between us, but she could see how terrified I was. She didn't question me, just made up the guest bed and insisted I stay the night.

I didn't sleep much that night, feeling constantly nauseous. Every sound, every creak of the house made me jump. . It was like something out of a nightmare, and I couldn't shake the feeling of those yellow eyes watching me.

The next morning, I called in sick to work. I couldn't bring myself to drive back down that road, not after what had happened. Nancy tried to reassure me, but I could see the fear in her eyes too. She offered to let me stay with her for a few days, and I gratefully accepted.

We decided to drive back to my house together, during the daylight, to pick up some of my things. The drive was tense, both of us scanning the sides of the road for any sign of the creature. But the daylight seemed to have chased away the shadows, and there was no sign of it.

We reached my house, and I quickly packed a bag. The house felt different, colder somehow. I couldn't shake the feeling that I was being watched. We didn't stay long, just long enough for me to grab what I needed.

I stayed with Nancy for the next few days, trying to go about my life as normally as possible. But the memory of that creature haunted me. I found myself jumping at the slightest thing. Nothing, and I mean nothing, has ever had such a negative impact on me. It was like it radiated evil or something.

I did some research, trying to find any explanation for what I had seen. There were stories, of course—tales of werewolves and other creatures that lurk in the night. But they were just stories, weren't they? I couldn't find anything that matched what I had seen, nothing that made sense.

After a week, I finally went back to work. I couldn't avoid my life forever. But I took a different route home, avoiding that stretch of road. I couldn't bring myself to drive down it again, not after what had happened.

It was during one of my late-night research sessions that I stumbled upon stories about the Michigan Dogman. At first, it sounded like another urban legend, but the more I read, the more I felt a chill of recognition. The descriptions matched what I had seen— a massive, wolf-like creature that could stand on two legs with glowing yellow eyes. I found reports dating back to the late 1800s, tales of encounters that were eerily similar to mine.

The Michigan Dogman was supposedly first reported in Wexford County in 1887. Since then, sightings have occurred sporadically across the state. People described the same sense of terror, the same glowing eyes, and the same inexplicable presence. Reading these accounts made my experience feel more real, but also more terrifying. I wasn't the only one who had seen this creature, and I certainly wouldn't be the last.

Dr. Collins, the therapist Nancy recommended, has been a great help. She's patient and understanding, never once making me feel silly for what I experienced. She's taught me techniques to manage my anxiety, to face my fears instead of letting them control me. It's a slow process, but I'm starting to feel like myself again.

I've also started keeping a journal, writing down my thoughts and feelings. It helps to get everything out on paper, to see my fears laid out in front of me. It's a way to confront the darkness, to take control of the narrative.

I've also found a community online, a group of people who have had similar experiences. It's comforting to know that I'm not alone, that others have seen things that defy explanation. We share our stories, offer support, and try to make sense of it all together.

One thing that's surprised me is the number of people who believe in the supernatural. I've always been a rational person, someone who trusts in science and logic. But my encounter has opened my eyes to the possibility that there's more to this world than we can see or understand.

I still have bad nights, times when the fear creeps back in and I can't shake the feeling of being watched. But those nights are becoming less frequent. The techniques Dr. Collins taught me are helping, and I'm slowly regaining my sense of normalcy.

Despite everything, I've decided not to move. My little house in the woods is still my home, and I refuse to let fear drive me away. I've made some changes, though. I installed better lighting around the property, and I'm considering getting a dog for companionship and security.

I've also reconnected with my love for nature. I go for walks in the woods during the day, finding comfort in the beauty of my surroundings. It's a way to reclaim the peace that the encounter tried to take from me.

Looking back, I realize how much that night changed me. I'm stronger now, more resilient. I've faced something terrifying and come out the other side. It hasn't been easy, but I'm learning to live with the fear, to accept it as part of my new reality.

CREATURES OF THE DARK AT FORT LEWIS

My name is Sergeant Jason Harlow, and I've served in the Army for nearly 27 years. I've seen and experienced things most people couldn't imagine, but what happened ten years ago at Fort Lewis, Washington, still haunts me to this day. The night we were ordered to hightail it out of there during a training exercise was unlike any other. This story has been eating at me for a long time, and I need to get it off my chest. Obviously, I have changed my name and those of my fellow officers.

It was a typical late October night, damp and chilly, with the kind of fog that rolls in and makes everything feel like it's wrapped in a wet blanket. My squad and I were part of a training exercise, nothing out of the ordinary, really. We were deep in the forest, playing the part of a rescue team searching for a downed pilot. Our boss, Captain Walker, was monitoring us via a drone equipped with thermal imaging.

We had been out there for hours, moving through the dense forest, communicating quietly through our headsets. The forest was alive with the sounds of nocturnal animals, but it was nothing we hadn't heard before. Our mission was straightforward: find the "downed pilot" and extract him safely.

Everything was going according to plan until we received an urgent call from Captain Walker. His voice crackled through our headsets, filled with an edge we hadn't heard before. "Sergeant Harlow, you need to hightail it outta there, pronto. You've got two large heat signatures coming your way."

I frowned and exchanged glances with my squad. We were wearing thermal gear ourselves, so if something was out there, we should've seen it too. "Sir, can you clarify? We're not picking up anything on our end," I replied, trying to keep my voice steady.

"You will soon. They're closing in on your position. I don't know what they are, but they're abnormally large—two to three times the size of your heat signatures."

"Should we engage, sir?" I asked.

"Negative, Sergeant. Make your way to the clearing ASAP."

A chill swept over me. The forest suddenly seemed much darker and more hostile. "Roger that, sir. We're moving out," I said, signaling to my squad to fall back. We started moving quickly but quietly, our senses working overtime. The forest, which had seemed merely damp and cold before, now felt suffocatingly oppressive. We were trained soldiers, but there was something about the urgency in Captain Walker's voice that had us all on edge.

As we made our way through the dense underbrush, the sounds started. At first, it was just an occasional rustling that we could attribute to small animals. But then it grew louder, more obvious. Heavy footsteps, the kind that didn't belong to any deer or bear. It felt like the forest itself was holding its breath, waiting for something to happen.

"Did you hear that?" Private Allen whispered, his voice barely audible.

I nodded, my grip tightening on my rifle. "Stay sharp and keep moving. We need to get out of here," I said, trying to keep my voice calm.

The sounds grew closer, more distinct. There was a strange clicking noise, almost like the sound of a giant insect. It was unsettling, to say the least. We picked up the pace, our breath visible in the cold night air. The fear was nearly suffocating, an unspoken understanding among us that we were not alone and whatever was out there was not friendly.

Captain Walker's voice came through the headset again, more urgent this time. "They're right on top of you. Move faster!"

We broke into a jog, trying to put as much distance between us and whatever was out there as possible. The sounds followed us, never getting closer but never falling behind either. It was like a game of cat and mouse, and we were the prey.

As we navigated through the underbrush, Private Allen suddenly froze, staring into the darkness. "Sarge, look!" he whispered urgently, pointing.

I turned to where he was pointing and saw it through the thermal—an enormous figure on its belly, crawling toward us like a spider. Its movements were unnaturally smooth and fluid, almost creepily supernatural. The creature was massive, easily twice the size of a large man, and covered in dark, matted hair that hung down at least three inches. It was the creepiest thing I have ever seen in my life.

I think my blood stopped flowing. "Captain Walker, we've got eyes on one of the heat signatures. We need an extraction team ASAP!" I shouted into my headset, trying to keep the panic out of my voice.

The growling and clicking grew louder, more insistent. It felt like we were surrounded, but there was nothing to be seen. The tension was overwhelming.

Not knowing who or what your enemy is not only dangerous but extremely anxiety-inducing.

We finally reached a clearing and paused to catch our breath. The forest around us was eerily silent. I checked in with Captain Walker. "Sir, we've reached a clearing. Any update on those heat signatures?"

"They've stopped moving, but they're still there. Hold your position for now and stay alert," he replied.

We formed a defensive perimeter, our eyes scanning the darkness for any sign of movement. The silence was deafening, each minute stretching into what felt like an hour. I had no idea what we were facing. What were those heat signatures? And what in the world was large enough to register as twice the size of a man?

Suddenly, the silence was broken by another low, growl mixed with a agonizingly drawn-out moan. I couldn't pinpoint exactly where it was coming from. I didn't think my heart could pound any faster, my body tense and ready for action. The growl was followed by the same strange clicking noises, like the sound of giant mandibles snapping shut.

"Eyes up! Stay sharp!" I barked, my voice steadier than I felt.

We scanned the tree line, our rifles at the ready. The growling and clicking grew louder, more pronounced. It felt like we were surrounded, but there was nothing to be seen.

Then all of a sudden the noise stopped. The forest was silent once more, like nothing had happened. We waited, our breaths shallow, our bodies taut with anticipation.

"Sergeant Harlow, the heat signatures are retreating," Captain Walker's voice came through the headset, filled with relief. "Hold your position. I'm sending an extraction team to your location."

We stayed in the clearing, our eyes never leaving the darkness. The relief was short-lived, the fear still lurking in the back of our minds. We only glimpsed what had been stalking us, but we had felt its presence, and it was something none of us would ever forget.

The extraction team arrived, and we were pulled out of the forest. Captain Walker debriefed us, but there were no answers, only more questions. What were those heat signatures? Why weren't we allowed to engage? And what had been making those sounds?

The official report chalked it up to a training exercise gone awry, an encounter with an unknown animal. But we knew better. There was something out there in the forest that night, something that defied explanation. It had watched us, followed us, and let us go.

Ten years later, it hasn't left my mind. Later, a few of my team discussed what it could have been and one of the men suggested a Sasquatch. I was reluctant to agree at the time but the more I looked into it, the more I believe that is what we encountered that night.

WILDLIFE BIOLOGIST ENCOUNTERS CREATURE

PENNSYLVANIA

As a wildlife biologist, I've spent my life exploring the woods and wild places of Pennsylvania. I've always found solace in the forests, with their towering trees, dense underbrush, and the cacophony of sounds that make up the natural world. My name is Louie, and what I experienced on a routine hike to a familiar spot has forever altered my understanding of what may exist in the wilderness.

It was early October, the time of year when the leaves turn brilliant shades of red, orange, and yellow. The air was clear and refreshing with no clouds in the sky—a perfect day for a hike. I had the weekend off and decided to take a trip to one of my favorite research spots deep in the Allegh-

135

eny National Forest. This particular area had always been rich with wildlife, and I hoped to gather some data for a project I was working on regarding local deer populations.

I packed my gear, including a camera, GPS, and field notebook, and set out early in the morning. The drive to the trailhead took about an hour, and by the time I arrived, the sun was just starting to break through the morning mist. I locked my car, slung my backpack over my shoulder, and began my hike into the forest.

The trail was familiar, one I had hiked countless times before. It wound through dense stands of hemlock and pine, past bubbling streams and over rocky outcrops. I took my time, enjoying the tranquility and the feeling of being alone in nature. The only sounds were the crunch of leaves underfoot and the occasional call of a distant bird.

After a couple of hours, I reached a clearing that over-looked a small valley. This spot had always been a favorite of mine. It offered a stunning view and was a great place to sit and observe wildlife. I took a seat on a fallen log, pulled out my notebook, and started jotting down observations.

That's when I noticed something unusual. At the far end of the clearing, near the edge of the tree line, there was movement. I squinted, trying to make out what it was. At first, I thought it might be a bear, but as the figure stepped into the open, I realized it was walking on two legs.

I couldn't move. The figure was tall, over eight feet, built like a bodybuilder with chestnut colored hair all over its body, except its face. Its arms looked unusually long and it had a small, somewhat cone-shaped head. It was definitely not something I'd ever seen in the animal kingdom. It moved with a calculated, almost human elegance.

I reached for my camera, my hands trembling. I managed to snap a few pictures before the creature seemed to notice me. It stopped, turning its head in my direction. A tingle of dread coursed through me as its eyes locked onto mine. They were black and overly large, yet filled with an intelligence and awareness that was unmistakably unsettling.

For a moment, neither of us moved. The forest around us seemed to go silent, the air heavy with tension. I could feel my breath quickening, my mind going a million miles an hour trying to process what this animal was. This couldn't be real. Sasquatch was a myth, a legend told around campfires. Yet here it was, standing no more than fifty yards away, looking right at me.

Suddenly, the creature emitted a deep, resonant vocalization—a cross between a roar and a grunt. It was a noise that reverberated through my body, filling me with a primal fear. I slowly rose to my feet, my instincts screaming at me to run, but my scientific curiosity keeping me rooted to the spot.

The creature stood there, watching me with those intense eyes. It began to sway from side to side, an unsettling motion that heightened my sense of dread. My heart pounded in my chest, and I could feel the sweat on my forehead despite the cool autumn air.

Then, without warning, the creature bellowed again and charged at me. It was a bluff charge, but it was enough to send me stumbling backward, my mind a whirlwind of fear and confusion. Just as quickly as it had charged, the creature stopped, turned, and ran back into the forest, disappearing with astonishing speed and agility.

I have never seen something move so fast in my life.

I stood there, stunned, my mind failing to process what had just happened. The clearing felt empty and silent, the tension slowly dissipating. My hands were shaking, and I realized I had been holding my breath. I took a deep breath, trying to calm my racing heart, but the encounter had left me shaken to my core.

I sat down on the log, my legs feeling like jelly. I needed to get back to my car, to safety, but I also needed to record everything I had seen. I took a deep breath, trying to calm my racing heart, and began writing furiously in my notebook. Every detail, every sensation, every emotion—I needed to capture it all before the memory faded.

The hike back to the trailhead was a blur. My senses were on high alert, every snap of a twig sending a jolt of adrenaline through my body. I kept glancing over my shoulder, half-expecting to see the creature following me, but the forest remained quiet and still.

When I finally reached my car, I felt a wave of relief wash over me. I climbed in, locked the doors, and sat there for a moment, trying to steady my nerves. I pulled out my camera and reviewed the pictures I had taken. They were blurry from my hands shaking, but there was no mistaking the tall, hairy figure in the frames.

I drove home in a daze, my mind replaying the encounter over and over. I needed to tell someone, to share what I had seen, but I also knew that most people would be skeptical, if not outright dismissive. Sasquatch sightings were the stuff of tabloid newspapers and conspiracy theories, not reputable scientific research.

Over the next few days, I poured over my notes and photos, trying to piece together a coherent account of the encounter. I reached out to a few colleagues who I trusted, sharing my story and my evidence. Their reactions were mixed—some were intrigued, others were skeptical—but all agreed that the photos were compelling.

Despite the skepticism, I knew what I had seen was real. I decided to write up my findings in a detailed report, documenting every aspect of the encounter. I included my photos, my field notes, and a thorough analysis of the evidence. It was a risk, putting my reputation on the line, but I felt it was important to share what I had experienced.

The report generated a lot of interest, both positive and negative. Some people were fascinated by the evidence and wanted to know more, while others dismissed it as a hoax or a misidentification. But the encounter had changed me, and I was determined to pursue the truth, no matter the cost.

I continued my research, spending more time in the field and gathering additional evidence. I set up trail cameras, collected hair samples, and interviewed other witnesses. The more I learned, the more convinced I became that there was something out there, something that science had yet to explain.

As a wildlife biologist, I've always been driven by a desire to understand the world around me. The encounter with the Sasquatch was a stark reminder that there are still mysteries out there, waiting to be uncovered. It reignited my passion for exploration and discovery, pushing me to look beyond the known and venture into the unknown.

The years since that day have been filled with research, exploration, and countless hours spent in the field. I've encountered skeptics and believers, faced criticism and support, but through it all, I've remained committed to finding the truth.

THE DAY AT CRYSTAL LAKES

My name is Johan, and I'm here to share an experience that still haunts me to this day. I visited my brother, Howie, in Boulder, Colorado, from September 19th through the 26th. Howie has a cabin up at Crystal Lakes, near Red Feather, Colorado, at an elevation above 8,500 feet. It's a place we've always loved for its peace, quiet, and excellent trout fishing. This trip, however, turned out to be anything but peaceful.

We arrived at his cabin on Sunday, excited for a week of fishing and enjoying the great outdoors. However, a sudden snowfall kept us inside for two and a half days. By Tuesday morning, the snow had finally stopped, and the world outside was covered in a pristine white blanket. It was around 7:30 AM when I stepped out onto the front porch, hoping to see some sign of life or, at the very least, get some fresh air.

I took in a deep breath of fresh air, the ground was glistening under the early morning sun. As I stood there, taking it all in, something caught my eye. About 100 yards away, near the edge of the aspen trees, I saw something. At first, I thought maybe it was a moose or a bear, but as I watched, I realized it was walking upright. It was black, tall, and moving steadily towards the trees. My heart just about leapt out of my chest.

I called out to Howie, who was inside making coffee. "Howie, come here! You've got to see this!" I grabbed the field glasses we always kept by the door for bird watching. Howie joined me on the porch, and I handed him the binoculars.

"What is it?" he asked, looking through the glasses.

"I don't know," I replied, my voice trembling. "But it's walking on two legs."

Howie adjusted the focus and gasped. "Johan, I think that's a Bigfoot."

We took turns watching the creature for several minutes. It was about 7 to 8 feet tall, with broad shoulders and a powerful build. I estimated it weighed around 350 to 400 pounds. The creature moved with purpose, seemingly startled by a pickup truck that had just come down the small dirt road leading to our cabin. It quickly disappeared into the aspen trees.

For a moment, we just stood there in stunned silence. Then, curiosity got the better of us. We grabbed the only measuring tool we had—a yardstick—and headed towards the spot where we had seen the creature. The snow was fresh and soft, making it easy to see any tracks.

When we reached the edge of the trees, we found the footprints. They were enormous, measuring 17 inches long and 6.5 inches wide. The sheer size of the prints sent a shiver down my spine. This was no bear or any other animal native to these parts. We knew we had to document it, so we carefully measured and took pictures with our phones.

We decided to follow the tracks, hoping to learn more about this mysterious creature. But as we moved deeper into the forest, the snow started to cover the prints. The further we went, the harder it became to follow the trail. After a while, the tracks vanished completely under the snow, leaving us standing in the middle of the forest with more questions than answers.

Howie and I looked at each other, the gravity of what we had just experienced sinking in. We decided to head back to the cabin, both of us feeling a strange mix of excitement and unease. As we walked back, we couldn't stop talking about what we had seen. Could it really have been a Sasquatch? The idea seemed ridiculous, yet the evidence was right there in front of us.

The rest of the day passed in a blur. We didn't feel much like fishing anymore. Instead, we stayed close to the cabin, keeping an eye on the woods and discussing what we should do next. Should we report it? Who would believe us? We knew that Bigfoot sightings were often met with skepticism and ridicule, but we also knew what we had seen.

That night, sleep did not come easily. Every little noise outside the cabin made me jump. The usual sounds of the forest, which I had always found soothing, now seemed ominous and threatening. I kept imagining those dark, intelligent eyes watching us from the trees, waiting for an opportunity to approach.

The next morning, we decided to venture out again, this time better prepared. We brought more measuring tools, a camera with a good zoom lens, and a notebook to document any findings. We headed back to the spot where we had found the footprints, but the overnight snowfall had covered any remaining evidence. We spent hours searching the area, hoping to find more tracks or some other sign of the creature, but our efforts were in vain.

We went about our activities—fishing, hiking, and enjoying the beautiful scenery—but the encounter was always in the back of our minds. We talked to a few locals, carefully gauging their reactions before mentioning what we had seen. Surprisingly, some of them didn't dismiss our story outright. There were whispers and rumors of strange sightings in the area, though no one had ever provided concrete evidence.

By the time my visit came to an end, I was eager to return home but also felt a strange sense of loss. I had always loved the mountains and forests of Colorado, but now they seemed different, filled with unknown dangers and mysteries. The encounter had changed the way I looked at the world, and I knew it would stay with me forever.

Back in Pennsylvania, I tried to settle back into my routine, but it wasn't easy. I found myself researching Bigfoot sightings, reading about other encounters, and trying to make sense of what we had seen. The scientific part of me wanted to find a logical explanation, but the evidence pointed to something beyond the realm of known wildlife.

DEER CHASING SASQUATCH

My name is Leona H., and I'm here to tell you about an experience that my family and I had on August 10th or 11th, 1990—I'm not sure of the exact date, but it was a Sunday at around 11:00 am on a bright, sunny day. We were in Larimer County, in the Roosevelt National Forest, about twenty-five miles northwest of Fort Collins. The nearest highway would be Hwy 34, which goes through Loveland, about 20 miles away. This story still gives me chills when I think about it, and I guarantee you, it's all true.

My son, Dallas C., his wife, a friend, and I had just bought a small piece of property in the area. We were busy building a bridge across Buckhorn Creek. It was a beautiful day, and we decided to take a break and enjoy the surroundings. Dallas was scanning a mountain to the west of us with his binoculars when he suddenly froze and whispered urgently for his wife to take a look.

She grabbed the binoculars and looked through them. Her face went pale, and she handed them back to me, exclaiming, "It's chasing some deer." Then she said, "My God, Mom, it's got knees!" Her voice was filled with a mix of awe and fear. I quickly took the binoculars and peered through them.

At first, I couldn't believe what I was seeing. There, running across the face of the mountain, was a creature that should not have been there. It was massive, with pitch-black fur that contrasted starkly with the bright daylight. Its gait was strange and distinctive, almost like it was gliding over the rugged terrain. It was incredibly fast, too fast to be a human, especially in that kind of environment.

The friend who was with us saw it without binoculars and was equally shocked. We stood there, silently watching as it disappeared into a group of pine trees. My heart was pounding, and I felt a mix of fear, excitement, and disbelief. We waited for several minutes, hoping to see it again.

Sure enough, it leaped out from the trees and started running across the rocky mountain face. I swear, that thing could run like the wind. It was breathtaking and terrifying at the same time. No human could run that fast, especially across that rugged mountain, and it had to be about 8 feet tall or more. It was definitely not a bear or any other animal we were familiar with.

What puzzled me was that this Sasquatch didn't fit with things I had read about them. Most descriptions mentioned a reddish-brown color, but this one was pitch black. It was seen in broad daylight, in the middle of the day, which also seemed unusual.

As we watched, a huge bird, maybe a vulture of some kind, kept circling around where the creature was. It was like the bird was waiting for the Sasquatch to make a kill. It was an eerie sight, adding to the surreal atmosphere of the moment.

Dallas insisted that the creature had a tuft of snow-white hair on its head, a detail that seemed almost too bizarre to be true, but he was adamant about it. We didn't report the sighting to anyone because we didn't think anybody would believe us, plus, we didn't want some gun-happy nuts trying to hunt it down.

My husband and I have been living out here on and off since that time and we've been staring at that mountain for years, but we've never seen another one. Never-the-less, I feel truly blessed to have witnessed such an incredible sight.

The property we bought is at about 6,500 feet elevation, and where we saw the Sasquatch was probably a few hundred feet higher. The area is rich with vegetation, pine trees, and numerous creeks and lakes. The spot where we saw it running was mostly bare and rocky, but it disappeared into a dense forest of pines.

That year, the area was pretty much wilderness, though it's more inhabited now. I've never heard of any other sightings around here, but nobody could ever convince us that we didn't see what we know we saw.

The sighting left us all in a state of shock. Even now, when I think back to that day, I get chills. Seeing something so inexplicable, something that defied all logic and understanding, was a profoundly humbling experience.

After the creature disappeared into the trees, we all just stood there, silent and stunned. The magnitude of what we had just witnessed was overwhelming.

Over the years, we've continued to visit the property. Every time we go, we can't help but look towards the mountain, hoping for another glimpse of the creature. But we've never seen it again. That one encounter remains etched in our memories.

My son, Dallas, took a particular interest in researching Sasquatch. He devoured books, documentaries, and articles, trying to piece together a comprehensive understanding of what we had seen. He even joined a few online communities dedicated to Bigfoot research. Through these groups, he found others who had similar experiences, and it was comforting to know we weren't alone.

I often reflect on what we saw and what it means. The Sasquatch, if that's indeed what it was, challenges our understanding of the natural world. It suggests that there are still undiscovered creatures, hidden in the remote corners of our planet. It's a humbling thought, one that fills me with a sense of wonder and curiosity.

KNOCK KNOCK KNOCK

I've lived in British Columbia my entire life, and the forests here have always been my sanctuary. My name is Dion, and at sixty years old, I've spent more time in these woods than I care to admit. There's a predictable dance of nature in the wilderness that's always brought me comfort. I thought I had seen it all, but I was very wrong.

It was late September, just a few hours before dark, when I decided to go for a walk. It was a nice night out, and the leaves were turning, painting the forest in vibrant shades of orange and red. I pulled on my jacket, grabbed my walking stick, and set off down the familiar trail behind my house. The sun was beginning its descent, casting shadows that danced across the forest floor.

About thirty minutes into my walk, I heard a distinct, sharp knock, like wood hitting wood. I stopped and listened, figuring it was just a tree branch falling or maybe an animal. But then it came again, louder this time. I glanced around, feeling a prickle of unease. It was strange, but I shrugged it off and kept walking.

As I continued, the knocks grew more frequent and seemed to follow me. Each step I took was met with a corresponding knock. I thought that was very strange and I soon felt like I wasn't alone out there. I quickened my pace, hoping to outdistance whatever was making the noise.

The deeper I went into the woods, the louder and more insistent the knocks became. It was as if the forest itself was trying to warn me. My heart started to race, and I felt a cold sweat trickle down my back. I wasn't just uneasy anymore—I was scared. Real fear, the kind that grips your chest and makes your legs feel like jelly.

I tried to rationalize it. Maybe it was a woodpecker, or some other animal making the noise. But deep down, I knew that wasn't it. No. This was deliberate. Intentional. Someone or something was out there, and it was following me.

The sun was sinking lower, and the shadows were growing longer. I knew I had to get back home before dark. The last thing I wanted was to be lost in the woods with whatever was making those knocks. I turned around and started heading back, my pace quickening with each step.

The knocks didn't stop. They seemed to match my

movements, getting louder and more frantic the closer I got to home. My breath came in short, panicked gasps, and I felt a rising sense of dread. What if I couldn't find my way back? What if I got turned around?

Finally, after what felt like hours, I broke through the tree line and saw my house. Relief washed over me, but it was short-lived. The knocking didn't stop. It echoed in the stillness, a relentless reminder that something was out there.

I rushed inside and locked the door, my heart still pounding in my chest. The knocks continued for a while, then slowly faded away. I sat in my living room, trying to calm myself down. I closed all the curtains and double-checked the locks, trying to create a barrier between myself and whatever was out there.

For the next few weeks, the knocks persisted. Every evening, just as the sun was setting, I would hear them. Sometimes they were distant, other times they sounded like they were right outside my window. I started to dread the coming of night, knowing that with the darkness would come the knocking.

One week after the knocks began, something happened that pushed me over the edge. I had a pile of lumber stacked near my back door, leftovers from a project I'd been working on. It was late, and I was sitting in my living room, trying to read and take my mind off the relentless knocks. That's when I heard it—a heavy, deliberate thud against the side of my house.

My heart leapt into my throat, and I froze. I could hear

something—or someone—picking up the pieces of lumber and throwing them against the house. The thuds were loud and menacing, shaking the walls and filling me with a primal fear. I wanted to get up, to look outside and see what was causing the noise, but I was too scared. I stayed where I was, too petrified to move, and prayed for the noise to stop.

The next morning, I cautiously stepped outside to inspect the damage. The lumber had been moved, scattered across the yard, and there, in the soft earth, were footprints. They were large, much larger than any human's, and they trailed off into the woods. I felt very uneasy, and I quickly went back inside, locking the door behind me.

After that night, the knocking stopped. The silence was almost more unsettling than the noise had been. It always felt like something was there and watching me, and every little sound made me jump. I started to feel like a prisoner in my own home, constantly on edge and waiting for the next terrifying encounter.

Within a year, I made the decision to move. I couldn't take it anymore. The fear had seeped into every corner of my life, and I knew I couldn't stay there. I sold the house and moved to a small apartment in the city, far away from the woods and the terror that had stalked me.

Looking back, I still don't know what it was that haunted me. Was it a person playing a cruel joke, or something else entirely? Whatever it was, it left a mark on me that I'll carry for the rest of my life.

DEPUTY'S SASQUATCH ENCOUNTER

ARKANSAS

My name is Art and I've been serving as a Deputy in the small town of Cedarville, Arkansas, for the better part of twenty years. Our town is nestled in the Ozarks, surrounded by large forests and hills. Life here is generally quiet, with the occasional small-town drama or wildlife disturbance. But I am here to tell you about a series of events that took place in the summer of 2010, events that I still can't believe happened to this day.

It started with a call from the Hensleys, an elderly couple who lived on the outskirts of town. Ed and Martha Hensley were in their late seventies and had been married for over fifty years. They were well-known in the community, respected and liked by everyone. So, when Ed called the station one hot July evening, claiming that something—or someone—was harassing them, I took it seriously.

"Deputy Reynolds, we've got something strange happening out here," Ed said, his voice shaky. "Martha and I have been hearing noises at night, and something has been getting up on the roof banging away. I think someone's out there, maybe even more than one person."

I assured Ed I'd be over to check things out. Cedarville didn't see much action, so dealing with potential trespassers or vandals was as serious as it got. I grabbed my flashlight and headed out to the Hensley place, which was about a fifteen-minute drive from the station.

The Hensleys' house was a modest, single-story home surrounded by thick woods. As I pulled up the gravel driveway, the sun was just going down. Ed was waiting for me on the porch, his face etched with worry.

"Thanks for coming, Art," he said, shaking my hand. "We've been hearing these noises for the past few nights—grunting, growling, and then there's the banging on the walls. It's scaring Martha half to death."

I nodded, feeling a twinge of concern. "Let's take a look around."

We walked the perimeter of the property, my flashlight cutting through the encroaching darkness. I didn't see anything out of the ordinary—no signs of forced entry, no footprints, no evidence of any intruders. I assured Ed that I'd keep an eye on things and told him to call me if anything else happened.

Over the next few days, I made it a point to drive by the Hensley place during my patrols. I even stopped by a few times to walk the property again, but I never saw or heard anything unusual. Ed and Martha seemed to relax a bit, thinking that maybe whatever it was had moved on.

But then, one night, everything changed.

It was a Friday evening, around 10 PM, when the call came in. Martha was on the line, her voice trembling with fear. "Art, please come quickly. It's back, and it won't leave us alone."

I jumped in my patrol car and sped over to the Hensley house. As I approached, I saw Martha standing on the porch, clutching a blanket around her shoulders. Ed was beside her, holding a shotgun. The fear in their eyes was evident.

"What happened?" I asked, stepping out of the car.

"It's out there, in the woods," Ed said, pointing towards the tree line. "We heard it howling, and then it started banging on the house again."

I grabbed my flashlight and unholstered my sidearm. "Stay here. I'm going to take a look."

I walked towards the woods, my heart pounding in my

chest. The night was eerily quiet, the only sound being the crunch of leaves under my boots. I swept the flashlight back and forth, scanning the darkness for any sign of movement.

As I ventured deeper into the woods, I started to hear something—a low, deep growl that stopped me in my tracks. I tried to pinpoint the direction it was coming from. Then, out of the corner of my eye, I saw a shadow move.

"Who's there?" I called out, my voice steady despite the adrenaline coursing through my veins. "This is Deputy Reynolds. Show yourself."

There was no response, only the continued growling. I took a step forward, and that's when I saw it.

Standing about thirty feet away was a massive form, had to be about 9 feet tall, 4 feet wide and covered in dense, dark hair. Its eyes reflected the beam of my flashlight, glowing with an eerie, red light. I couldn't fathom what my eyes were seeing—part man, part beast. A Sasquatch, if you will.

My breath caught in my throat, and for a moment, I couldn't move a muscle. The creature stared at me, its eyes locked onto mine. Then, with a sudden, powerful movement, it let out a deafening roar and charged towards me.

Instinct took over. I fired a warning shot into the air, hoping to scare it off. The creature stopped instantly, snarling at me. I slowly backed away, keeping my flashlight and gun trained on it. After what felt hours, the Sasquatch turned and disappeared into the darkness of the woods.

I stood there, trembling, my heart racing. What the hell had I just seen? I knew I had to get back to the Hensleys and make sure they were safe.

When I returned to the house, Ed and Martha were waiting anxiously on the porch. "Did you see it?" Ed asked, his voice filled with a mix of fear and curiosity.

I nodded, still trying to catch my breath. "Yeah, I saw it. And it's definitely not human."

We spent the rest of the night inside the house, with all the lights on and the doors locked. I stayed with the Hensleys until morning, keeping watch and trying to figure out what had just happened. The creature didn't return, but the memory of its glowing eyes and powerful presence was burned into my mind.

Over the next few days, I couldn't get the encounter out my mind.

Despite the lack of concrete evidence, I knew what I had seen was real. The Hensleys were convinced too, and they decided to stay with their daughter in Little Rock for a while, just to be safe.

I continued my patrols, always keeping a watchful eye on the woods, but I never saw the creature again. The nights were quieter, the disturbances at the Hensley place ceased, and life slowly returned to normal.

Ed and Martha came back from Little Rock, and we

all tried to put the encounter behind us. But it was always there, lurking in the back of our minds. Every now and then, Ed would call me, just to chat and to reassure himself that everything was still calm and quiet.

I spent more time patrolling the woods, especially at night. The encounters made me more attuned to the sounds and rhythms of the forest. I learned to distinguish between the natural noises of wildlife and something more unusual. But the creature never reappeared, and the nights grew quieter as summer turned to fall.

I also took up hiking as a hobby, partly as a way to explore the woods more thoroughly and partly to confront my lingering fear. I wanted to understand the environment better, to feel more connected to the land where such a mysterious creature could exist. It was a therapeutic process, one that helped me find some peace of mind.

I also found myself becoming an unofficial spokesperson for Sasquatch sightings in the area. People who had their own experiences but were too afraid to speak up began coming to me, sharing their stories. Some were clearly fabrications, but others had a ring of truth to them. It was comforting to know that I wasn't alone, that others had seen things they couldn't explain.

SASQUATCH HARASSES TEENS

My name is Jeff, and I'm now 38 years old, living a quiet life in Washington state. What I'm about to share is a story from my youth, a night that I'll never forget. I was a young teen in junior high school at the time, and though it's been years, the details of that encounter remain vivid, etched into my memory like it happened just yesterday.

It was a typical Friday night, and my parents had gone out, leaving me and my friend Scott alone at the house. Scott was my best friend, always cracking jokes and playing pranks. We were both aspiring wrestlers, dedicated to our training, and neither of us drank or used drugs. We were just good kids enjoying a night of freedom.

We had been watching TV in the living room, the only light coming from the flickering screen. The front door was a few feet away, and behind it, the dark, quiet night of our rural neighborhood. It was close to midnight when Scott, ever the kidder, suddenly got this look on his face and pointed towards the front door.

"Hey Jeff, I think someone's out there," he said, half-laughing.

I rolled my eyes, ready to call his bluff. "Yeah, right," I replied, standing up to prove him wrong. But as I approached the door, my stomach did black flips. There, through the small window at the top of the door, was a face. A grotesque face.

At first, I thought it was another one of Scott's pranks. But as I got closer, I realized this was no joke. The head looking in at us was something from a nightmare—dark, round, almost like a coconut, but with a menacing presence. The eyes were piercing, almost human-like that sent a wave of fear through my entire body.

We freaked out, with both of us bolting into my mom's bedroom, our hearts about to explode. We grabbed my dad's old .22 rifle and hurriedly loaded it with bullets. My hands were shaking so badly that it took me a moment to get it done.

"Scott, go lock the door," I urged, but he shook his head vehemently.

"No way," he whispered back, his face pale with fear. So we stayed in the bedroom, which at the time didn't have any curtains. The only barrier between us and the outside was the thin glass of the window.

Then we heard breathing. Heavy, labored breathing, like something massive was just outside. The sound was accompanied by a scratching noise, like claws against the window frame. And then we saw a large, hairy hand pressing up against the screen. It was enormous, easily covering half the window. From the angle, it had to be at least 8 to 10 feet tall to be looking in like that.

My whole body was shaking as I raised the rifle. I could barely breathe, let alone aim properly. Scott stood beside me, his eyes about to pop out of his head. The creature's face came into view again, and it was even more horrifying up close—large, black, and hairy, with red glowing eyes.

"Shoot it, Jeff," Scott urged, his voice barely a whisper.

I took a deep breath and squeezed the trigger. The shot rang out, deafening in the confined space of the bedroom. But I missed. The creature didn't flinch; it just stared at us with those unnerving eyes.

"Again," Scott said, more urgently this time. He grabbed the rifle from me and fired another shot. This time, the creature roared and took off running, its footsteps pounding the ground like thunder.

We stood there, stunned and trembling, the silence

that followed almost as terrifying as the encounter itself. We called the sheriff, our voices shaking as we explained what had happened. When he arrived, he was skeptical, of course. He found the two bullet holes in the window but no blood, no footprints on the hard ground.

"Have you boys been drinking?" he asked, eying us suspiciously.

"No, sir," I replied, still shaken. "We're wrestlers. We don't drink or use drugs."

The sheriff seemed to believe us, but there was little he could do. He took our statements and left, leaving Scott and me to deal with the aftermath. When my parents and brother came home, they found us huddled together, scared to death. My brother noticed the impression of the large hand on the window screen.

My parents believed us, but there was a sense of helplessness. What could they do against something like that? Scott and I tried to go back to our normal lives, but we avoided the woods, stayed indoors more, and rarely talked about that night.

Years passed, and Scott tragically passed away in a car accident shortly after we graduated high school. I often wonder if he ever really got over that night. As for me, I've moved on, built a life, but I will never forget that night.

THE HAUNTING OF BEAVER CREEK STATE PARK

OHIO

I'm a photographer based in northeast Ohio where work often takes me into the wilderness, capturing the beauty and serenity of nature. Photography has always been my escape, a way to connect with the world on a deeper level. Though, there is one encounter I had that changed the way I see those peaceful landscapes now. It was an encounter so strange and terrifying that I've hesitated to share it until now.

It was a beautiful afternoon in April. I had decided to visit Beaver Creek State Park, one of my favorite spots for capturing the fall foliage. The park, with its dense forests and meandering trails, has always been a haven for me. The rustling leaves and the gentle murmur of the creek create a symphony that soothes the soul. But that day, something felt off from the start.

I regret listening to my gut.

I parked my car at the usual spot, slung my camera bag over my shoulder, and set off down one of the lesser-used trails. The air was cool, and the sky was a brilliant blue. I wandered deeper into the woods, snapping photos of the vibrant reds, oranges, and yellows that adorned the trees.

As I reached a clearing, I paused to adjust my camera settings. Next thing I hear a low, mournful howl that sounded kind of like a siren. At first, I thought it might be a coyote, but it sounded like whatever was making the sound had a very large set of lungs. It was deep, almost human in its sadness.

I stood still, listening intently. The howl came again, followed by a series of guttural moans. *What the heck was this*, I thought. I've spent countless hours in the woods, and I've heard all sorts of wildlife, but this was different. It felt...otherworldly.

I wanted to believe it was just my imagination, but the sounds continued, growing louder and more intense. I scanned the area with my camera, hoping to catch a glimpse of whatever was making the noise, but there was nothing. Just the trees and the underbrush, swaying gently in the breeze.

After a few minutes, the sounds stopped as abruptly as they had started. The silence that followed was deafening. I stood there, heart pounding, trying to figure out what I had heard. I considered leaving, but curiosity got the better of me. I decided to continue my hike, hoping to find some rational explanation.

Yeah, I've been called stubborn more than a few times in my life.

The rest of the afternoon was uneventful. I took some beautiful shots of the fall scenery and tried to put the strange sounds out of my mind. But as I was packing up my gear to head home, I looked around feeling like someone was behind me. It was an unsettling sensation, as if unseen eyes were following my every move.

I tried to ignore it and started up a familiar hill, camera in hand, when that same sense of unease washed over me. The hairs on the back of my neck stood up, and my pulse quickened. I stopped and looked around, but there was no one else in sight. The trail was empty, and the spider webs stretched across it indicated that no one had passed through that morning.

I continued walking, but my steps were slow and cautious. Every snap of a twig, every small noise made me jump. As I neared the top of the hill, I heard the howls again—those same mournful cries that had haunted me earlier in the day. They were closer this time, more urgent and insistent.

Panic set in. I turned and started back down the trail, moving as quickly as I could without breaking into a run. The howls followed me, echoing through the trees. I glanced over my shoulder, half-expecting to see some monstrous figure looming behind me, but there was nothing. Just the empty trail and the silent woods.

By the time I reached my car, I was breathless and drenched in sweat. I jumped in, locked the doors, and sat there for a moment, trying to calm my racing heart. As I drove away, I couldn't shake the feeling that I had narrowly escaped something sinister, something I couldn't comprehend.

I avoided Beaver Creek State Park for a while after that. I focused on other projects, other locations.

One night, as I was going through my photos from that April day, I noticed something odd in one of the shots. In the background, among the trees, there was a dark shape, barely visible but definitely there. My heart skipped a beat. I zoomed in, but the image was too grainy to make out any details. Still, it was enough to reignite my curiosity—and my fear.

Despite my apprehension, I knew I had to go back. I needed answers, or at least some closure. Armed with my camera, a voice recorder, and a healthy dose of caution, I returned to Beaver Creek State Park on a warm afternoon in late May.

The park was quiet, as always. I followed the same trail,

my senses on high alert. Every sound, every movement caught my attention. I felt like a hunter, stalking my prey, but also like the hunted, aware that something could be watching me.

I reached the top of the hill and stopped, listening. The air was still, the silence oppressive. I pulled out my voice recorder and started talking, describing my surroundings, the sounds I had heard before, and the unease that gripped me. I felt a bit foolish, but it was comforting to have some form of documentation.

As I stood there, I noticed a faint, almost imperceptible smell—something musky and earthy, like wet fur and decaying leaves. It was faint, but distinct enough to make my stomach churn. I scanned the area with my camera, snapping photos in every direction.

And suddenly I heard a gruff sound, coming from somewhere behind me. I spun around, my heart racing. The gruff came again, louder this time, followed by a rustling in the underbrush. I raised my camera, snapping photos blindly as I backed away.

Then the sounds just stopped. The forest was silent once more, but the sense of being watched was overwhelming. I decided it was time to leave. I walked quickly but carefully down the trail, glancing over my shoulder every few steps.

When I reached my car, I didn't waste any time. I jumped in, started the engine, and drove away, my hands shaking on the steering wheel. I felt a mix of relief and frustration—relief that I was safe, but frustration that I still didn't have any clear answers.

Back at home, I reviewed the photos I had taken. Most were just trees and shadows, but one image stood out. In the background, partially obscured by the foliage, was a dark figure. It was indistinct, but it had the rough shape of a tall, broad-shouldered creature. My mind raced with possibilities, but I knew I had to be cautious. It could be a trick of the light, a misinterpretation of shadows.

I sent the photo to a few colleagues and friends, asking for their opinions. Most were skeptical, suggesting it was just pareidolia—the tendency to see familiar patterns, like faces, in random objects. But a couple of people saw what I saw—a large, humanoid figure lurking in the trees.

I also reviewed the audio from my voice recorder. The huffs were faint but audible, and there were other strange noises too—rustling, snapping branches, and an occasional low moan. It was enough to convince me that something was out there, something that didn't belong.

Unsure of what to do next, I reached out to a local cryptozoology group. They were intrigued by my story and the evidence I had gathered. We arranged to meet and discuss my encounters in more detail. It was a relief to talk to people who didn't dismiss me as crazy, who took my experiences seriously.

The group suggested a more thorough investigation

of Beaver Creek State Park. They planned to bring equipment—night vision cameras, audio recorders, and motion sensors. I agreed to join them, though the thought of going back still filled me with dread.

The night of the investigation was clear and moonlit. We met at the park entrance, a small group of us, armed with equipment and a shared sense of anticipation. As we walked the trails, the familiar sense of unease returned, but this time, I wasn't alone.

We set up camp near the top of the hill, the same place where I had heard the howls and growls. The team spread out, setting up cameras and sensors, while I stayed close to the fire, my heart pounding with a mix of fear and excitement.

Hours passed with no activity. We took turns keeping watch, scanning the darkness for any sign of movement. Around midnight, just as I was beginning to think we wouldn't find anything, the silence was shattered by a series of loud, mournful howls. The same howls that had haunted me for months.

The group sprang into action, recording the sounds and scanning the area with night vision cameras. The howls continued, growing louder and more insistent. I felt sick as I listened, the memories of my previous encounters flooding back.

Then, one of the motion sensors went off, a faint beep cutting through the night. We turned our attention to the direction of the alert, our cameras and flashlights trained on the darkness.

We scanned the area throughly, but didn't see the creature. After that, the howls and sounds tapered off and we walked back to the parking lot, after packing up.

As a photographer, I've always sought to capture the beauty of nature, but now, I also seek to understand its mysteries. The experiences at Beaver Creek State Park have taught me to look beyond the surface, to listen to the stories the land has to tell.

BIGFOOT ON THE TRACKS

OHIO

As it sit here thirty-one years later, what happened to me and my friend back in 1993 is as clear in my memory as if it happened yesterday. It was around August or September when we decided to take a walk down some railroad tracks near the Ohio River. My friend, Will, and I often went for an evening walk, the world quieting down as the sun dipped below the horizon. This particular walk, however, changed everything for me.

We started our walk from East Liverpool to Wellsville, Ohio, just below Route 7. The sun was setting, casting long shadows and painting the sky in hues of orange and pink. It must have been around 7:30 or 8:00 PM. The air was still warm, a lingering gift of summer, and the rhythmic crunch of our footsteps on the gravel was the only sound breaking the evening's stillness.

As we walked, we chatted about everything and nothing, the way old friends do. We had been friends since grade school, and these walks were a tradition for us. But that night, as we got about half a mile in, something felt off. The atmosphere seemed to change, becoming heavier somehow. It was then that we heard a noise—an unmistakable sound of brush being stomped down on the side of the hill to our right.

We stopped in our tracks and looked up. About 45 yards away, there stood an enormous figure, partially obscured by the trees. My heart skipped a beat as I tried to make sense of what I was seeing. It was leaning out from behind a tree, one massive arm wrapped around the trunk. It was covered in hair and incredibly tall, with big, muscular arms.

The creature had a presence, a sense of awareness that was almost human-like.

Then reality hit us like a freight train. We turned and ran as fast as we could. My heart was pounding, my legs were moving on autopilot, driven by pure fear. I didn't look back, too afraid of what I might see.

I could hear Bill's breath coming in ragged gasps beside me, matching the pounding of my own heart.

We didn't stop running until we were back in East Liverpool, our chests heaving and our legs trembling. We tried to process what we had seen, but it was too much. When

I told my parents about it later, they just laughed and dismissed it as nonsense. They said there was no such thing as Bigfoot. But I knew what I had seen, and so did Bill.

For years, I kept the memory to myself, sharing it only with a few trusted friends. Even now, decades later, it still seems surreal to me. It was real, and it was terrifying.

I believe in Bigfoot and believe that they are descendants of cavemen that have never evolved. And every time I think back to that night, I'm reminded of how little we truly understand about the world around us.

A SHADOW MOVING THROUGH THE TREES

WISCONSIN

Growing up in a small town in Wisconsin, I've always felt at home in the quiet, familiar surroundings. My name's Adam, and I've lived here my whole life. Over the years, I've seen my fair share of strange things, but absolutely nothing could have prepared me for what happened to me about three years ago. I was twenty at the time, living in a semi-rural house. We had neighbors on either side, but behind our place was a stretch of wildlife area—thick woods and marshland that seemed to go on forever.

It was late February, and the nights were starting to get a little warmer. I remember it was a Friday night because I had just gotten off work and decided to go out for a few drinks with some friends. By the time I left the bar, I wasn't drunk, but I had a nice buzz going. I decided to walk to the drug store to grab some aspirin and snacks before heading home. The store was only a short distance away, and I figured the fresh air would do me good.

The sky was clear, and the moon was bright, casting an eerie glow over everything. I walked along the quiet streets, enjoying the peace and quiet. I nodded to a few neighbors who were out, but most of the houses were dark and quiet. It was getting late, and people had already turned in for the night.

As I turned onto the path that led through the wildlife area, I felt a chill that had nothing to do with the temperature. It was like someone had walked over my grave. I shook it off and kept walking, telling myself I was just being paranoid. But then I heard movement coming from the bushes to my left.

At first, I thought it was just a deer or maybe a raccoon, but it sounded like it came from an animal larger than that. It was like something was following me, matching my pace step for step. I quickened my stride, trying to put some distance between myself and whatever was out there.

I was about halfway through the wildlife area when I saw it. At first, it was just a shadow moving between the trees, but as it got closer, I could see more details. It was massive, standing on two legs like a man but covered in long, dark fur. Its eyes glowed a yellow/amber color, and its snout was long and pointed, like a wolf's.

This can't be real, I thought. Every instinct screamed at me to run, but my legs felt bolted to the ground. The creature stopped about twenty feet away and just stared at me, its eyes burning into mine. I could see its breath steaming in the cold air, and I could hear a low growl rumbling from its chest.

This thing looked and felt evil to me but I just couldn't look away. Finally, my survival instincts kicked in, and I turned and ran as fast as I could. I didn't hear it chasing me but I wasn't go to hang around to find out.

I didn't stop until I burst through the back door of my house, slamming it shut behind me. I nearly busted it off its hinges. I locked every door and window, my heart pounding so hard I thought it might burst. I could now hear the creature outside, walking around. I didn't sleep at all that night, too terrified that it might break in. It was the most anxious night of my life.

The next morning, I went outside to see if there was any evidence of what had happened. The ground was torn up where I had seen the creature, and there were deep claw marks on the trees. I found huge footprints in the soft earth, but I didn't stick around to investigate further. I didn't want to risk another encounter.

For weeks after that night, I was on edge. Every time I went outside, I looked around for it. I stopped going for walks at night and made sure to stay inside after dark.

It's been three years since that night, and I still think about it all the time. I never saw the creature again, and part of me is grateful for that. But another part of me wonders what it was, and why it was following me. I've read stories about Dogman sightings in Wisconsin, but I never believed them until now.

HOWLS & SCREAMS ON OUR CAMPING TRIP

Howdy folks, name's Brad, and I'm fixin' to tell y'all about a campin' trip me and my family took that we'll never forget. We're from the great state of Texas, and this happened a few years back when we decided to spend a weekend out in the wilderness. We packed up our gear, loaded the kids into the truck, and set off for a good old-fashioned adventure with my brother's family. We had no idea what we were in for.

It was a beautiful Friday afternoon when we pulled into the campsite. The smell of pine was all around us. We picked a nice spot down by a creek, with plenty of room for the kids to run around and explore. My brother, Wes, and his wife, Cindy, set up their tent next to ours, and we got the fire pit ready for some evening s'mores.

The kids were excited as all get-out, runnin' around, collectin' sticks, and chattin' about the fun they were gonna have. My wife, Marla, and Cindy got to work on dinner, while Wes and I cracked open a couple of cold ones and set up the tents. The sun was settin', castin' a golden glow over the valley, and we were all lookin' forward to a peaceful night under the stars.

After a hearty dinner and some gooey s'mores, we all gathered around the campfire, tellin' stories and laughin' like we hadn't a care in the world. The kids' faces were illuminated by the flickering flames, their eyes wide with excitement as Tom spun a tall tale about a legendary creature that roamed these parts. We didn't think much of it, just good fun to get the kids' imaginations runnin'.

As the night wore on, the kids started to yawn, and we decided it was time to hit the hay. We tucked them into their sleeping bags, kissed them goodnight, and settled into our tents. The fire died down to glowing embers, and the sounds of the forest began to lull us to sleep.

It must've been around midnight when I was jolted awake by a sound that froze my blood. Screamin'. Not just one scream, but multiple, all at the same time. It was like a chorus of pure terror, echoing through the valley. I shot up, my heart poundin', and looked over at Marla, who was sittin' up, her eyes wide with fear.

"Brad, what the heck is that?" she whispered, her voice tremblin'.

"I don't know, but stay here with the kids," I said, grabbin' my flashlight and crawlin' out of the tent. Wes was already outside, anxiety etched into his face.

"You hear that?" he asked, his voice barely above a whisper.

"Yeah, it's comin' from down the valley," I replied, shinin' my flashlight into the darkness. The screams continued, a mix of high-pitched wails and deep, guttural howls. It was madness, chaos, like nothin' I'd ever heard before.

"What do you think it is?" Wes asked, his eyes dartin' around nervously.

"Coyotes," I said, though I didn't believe it for a second. "Probably just a pack of coyotes."

We stood there for a few more minutes, listenin' to the horrific sounds. The kids were stirrin' in the tents, and I knew we had to reassure them. "Let's get back inside and calm the kids down," I said. "We'll keep an eye out."

We crawled back into our tents and told the kids it was just some coyotes makin' noise. They seemed to buy it, but I could see the fear in their eyes. Marla looked at me, worry all over her face, but I gave her a reassuring nod. We lay there, listenin' as the screams continued, until suddenly, after about ten minutes, they stopped. Just like that. Silence.

We tried to go back to sleep, but I couldn't shake the uneasy feelin' in my gut. About twenty minutes later, just as I was startin' to drift off, I heard heavy footsteps, comin' down from the mountain. Whatever it was, it was big, and it wasn't tryin' to hide its presence.

I held my breath, listenin' as the footsteps got closer and closer. They were slow like something was takin' its time. I glanced over at Marla, who was wide awake, her eyes filled with fear. "Do you hear that?" she whispered.

"Yeah," I replied, my voice barely audible.

The footsteps entered our camp, and I could hear whatever it was movin' around. It walked over to the cooler, sniffed around, and I heard the lid creak open. My heart was doing backflips, and I felt a cold sweat break out all over me. I was too scared to move, too scared to even breathe.

After a while, the footsteps started to move away. I heard it walkin' back into the woods, and the sounds gradually faded into the distance. I lay there, frozen with fear, until the first light of dawn began to creep into the tent.

When the sun finally rose, we crawled out of our tents, exhausted and on edge. Wes and I examined the camp, lookin' for any signs of what had visited us during the night. The cooler had been opened, but nothin' was taken. There were no tracks, no clues, just the memory of those heavy footsteps and the terrifying screams.

We decided to cut the trip short and pack up. The kids

were quiet, clearly still shaken by the night's events. It was the fastest time our family has ever packed the car.

Whenever I think back on that trip, I can still hear the screams, still feel the ground tremble beneath those heavy footsteps.

That's my story, folks. Believe it or not, it's the God's honest truth.

CEDAR THICKET ENCOUNTER

OHIO

I'm a minister by profession, and I consider myself a rational, level-headed man. I've spent countless hours in the woods, finding solace and connection with nature, especially during deer hunting season. However, what I saw one November morning changed the way I see the world forever. This is my story.

It was a freezing morning, around 7:30 to 8:00 AM. The temperature was well below freezing, and a thin layer of snow blanketed the ground, crunching softly under my boots as I walked. I was deer hunting, sitting on an old road in the head of a hollow, watching a clearing between two cedar thickets. The clearing was about 50 or 60 yards across, with the thickets forming a natural barrier on either side.

I had chosen this spot because it offered a perfect vantage point. I was about a hundred yards from the trail crossing the clearing, hoping to catch sight of a deer as it ventured out. The morning was still, the only sounds were the occasional flutter of the leaves and the distant call of a crow. It was peaceful, almost serene.

That peace was shattered suddenly. From the top of the thicket to my left, I heard a crashing noise, the sound of brush and limbs breaking loudly, like large limbs being snapped. It lasted maybe ten seconds, a cacophony that seemed out of place in the stillness of the morning. I gripped my rifle a little tighter, scanning the thicket for any sign of movement.

Five minutes passed. Then, I heard the same noise again, this time about fifty to seventy-five feet down the hill, in the direction of the clearing. The crashing, thrashing, and breaking of limbs was unmistakable. It was as if something very large was moving through the thicket with incredible force. I strained my ears and eyes, trying to make sense of it.

Another five minutes passed, and the noise came again, closer still. This time it was about twenty yards into the thicket from the clearing. My nerves were on edge, my senses heightened. Then, out of the thicket stepped something that defied all reason.

It was walking on two legs, covered in black hair from head to toe. It had long arms that swung by its sides as it moved. The creature walked across the clearing in no more than five or six seconds, moving with a fluidity and speed that left me paralyzed with fear. I was too scared to move, too shocked to even raise my rifle.

I watched, stunned, as it disappeared into the thicket on the other side. My thoughts swirling with fear and confusion. It wasn't a bear; it walked upright like a man but was much larger and covered in thick, black hair. As the seconds dragged on, I finally forced myself to move. I took my gun and eased out of there, too busy watching the clearing to really look for tracks, though the thick grass would have hidden any anyway.

When I reached the truck, my heart was still racing. I waited anxiously for my hunting partner, Abe, worried that something might have happened to him.

As I stood by the truck, I kept thinking of the creature, every detail as clear as day. The way it moved, the sheer size of it—there was no mistaking it for anything other than what it was. But what was it? My thoughts were a whirlwind of fear and curiosity.

After about 30 minutes, I saw Abe coming out of the woods, looking none the worse for wear. He asked if I had seen a large pile of feces in the road through the clearing on my way out. I told him I hadn't.

He said it was right in the area where I saw the creature cross. He described the feces as loose, with grass and long, black hairs in it. I then told him what I had seen. Abe shook his head and said he was sure it was just a bear and my imagination had added the rest. He never did believe me, and neither has anyone else I've told. But I know what I saw, and it was no bear.

Abe led me to the spot where he had found the pile of feces. It was right in the middle of the path, exactly where I had seen the creature cross. The feces was unlike anything I had ever seen before. It was loose, mixed with grass, and contained long, black hairs. It seemed too large and unusual for any of the local wildlife. Abe still insisted it was just a bear, but I knew better.

We didn't have the tools to collect a sample, and neither of us had the expertise to analyze it. But the sight of it reinforced my belief that what I had seen was real. It was a physical manifestation of the creature's presence, something tangible that connected to my terrifying experience. Despite Abe's skepticism, I couldn't deny the evidence before me.

As a minister, faith is a central part of my life. My encounter in the woods challenged my understanding of the natural world, but it also deepened my faith. It humbled me, made me appreciate the vastness and complexity of creation.

I began incorporating these themes into my sermons, sharing the story of my encounter as a testament to the mysteries of the world and the importance of faith. Some members of my congregation were skeptical, but others found it inspiring. It was a way to bridge the gap between the known and the unknown, to embrace the mysteries of faith and the natural world.

Despite the passage of time, my curiosity about that morning never waned. I continue to hunt and explore the woods, always on the lookout for any sign of the creature. Each outing was is a mix of anticipation and fear and I hope one day, I see it again.

A MONSTER GRABBED MY FRIEND

I'm Sean, and I've lived in British Columbia for pretty much all of my 59 years. I grew up in Hope, BC, a small town nestled in the heart of the province's stunning wilderness. It was a peaceful place, surrounded by thick forests, beautiful mountains, and crystal-clear creeks. But let me tell you what my best friend Martin and I experienced one day, that I have never forgotten.

It was a warm summer afternoon when Martin and I decided to head down to the creek behind my house. We were thirteen at the time, and the creek was our playground. We'd spend hours there, catching frogs, skipping stones, and building makeshift dams. But that day, we got bored quicker than usual and decided to head home.

The walk back was uneventful at first. We chatted about school, our favorite TV shows, and what we planned to do over the weekend. The sun was starting to dip behind the trees, casting long shadows on the forest floor.

As we walked, we began to hear strange noises coming from the trees. It started as a faint rustling, but quickly grew louder. We stopped and listened, trying to figure out what it was. The sound was unusual—an eerie, almost rhythmic shaking.

Then, to our horror, we saw a tree being violently shaken. The entire trunk swayed back and forth as if some immense force was gripping it. Martin and I looked at each other, our eyes wide with fear. Without saying a word, we turned and started to run.

We sprinted through the forest, our hearts beating out of our chests. I could hear Martin's footsteps right behind me, the sound of twigs snapping and leaves crunching underfoot. Then all of a sudden his footsteps stopped, replaced by a loud, piercing scream. I turned around just in time to see Martin being grabbed by something massive and hairy. It lifted him off the ground and hurled him into the bushes with terrifying strength.

I didn't stop running. I was too scared, too frantic to think of anything but getting help. I burst through the trees and into my backyard, screaming for my dad. He was working on his car, covered in grease, but the moment he heard my screams, he dropped everything and ran towards me.

"What's wrong, Sean?" he shouted, worry all over his face.

"It's Martin! Something grabbed him!" I panted, barely able to catch my breath. "We need to help him!"

Without a second thought, my dad grabbed a wrench and ran back into the woods with me. We found Martin lying in the bushes, clutching his arm in pain. His face was streaked with tears, and he was trembling all over.

"What happened, son?" my dad asked gently, kneeling beside Martin.

"The... the monster grabbed me," Martin stammered, his voice shaking. "A big, hairy arm. It grabbed me and threw me."

We rushed Martin to the hospital, where the doctors confirmed that his arm was broken. While they were setting the bone and putting on a cast, my dad called the sheriff. We recounted the story, describing the noises, the tree shaking, and the attack. The sheriff listened carefully, but he seemed skeptical.

"Sounds like a bear to me," he said, scratching his head. "They can be pretty aggressive, especially if they feel threatened."

"But it wasn't a bear," Martin insisted, his voice firm despite his fear. "Bears don't have arms like that. This was something else."

The sheriff just nodded and took some notes, but it was clear he didn't believe us. To him, we were just a couple of kids with overactive imaginations.

A few years later, my family moved away from Hope. The memories of that day stayed with me, but life went on. I lost contact with Martin, and we never spoke about the incident again. But every now and then, I'd think about that hairy arm, the way it lifted Martin like he weighed nothing, and I'd shiver.

THE VISITOR IN THE NIGHT

WASHINGTON

My husband Theo and I own a cabin nestled deep in the woods of Washington State. It's a tranquil, secluded spot, perfect for those who seek peace and solitude away from the bustle of city life. Our cabin is our little own sanctuary, a place where we can disconnect from the world and enjoy the beauty of nature. That is until one night in the dead of winter, our peaceful retreat was shattered by an encounter that still wakes me up in a cold sweat.

It was early February, and the snow lay thick and undisturbed around our cabin. The temperature had plummeted, and the world outside was a silent, frozen expanse. We had spent the day chopping wood, securing the cabin against the biting cold, and had finally settled in for the evening. Theo was dozing in front of the TV, the soft glow flickering across his face, while I finished up some chores in the kitchen.

Around midnight, I noticed an odd odor wafting in from outside. It was faint at first, but distinctly unpleasant, like a mix of wet fur and decay. I wrinkled my nose, dismissing it as a passing animal, perhaps a bear recently roused from hibernation. I closed the window and curtains, trying to shut out the unsettling feeling that had started to creep over me, and decided to call it a night.

As I lay in bed, the cabin was eerily quiet, the kind of silence that makes every little creak and groan seem amplified. I must have drifted off to sleep because the next thing I knew, I was jolted awake by a loud metallic bang coming from the back porch. My heart jumped out of my chest as I strained to listen, every nerve in my body on high alert.

Then I heard the unmistakable sound of footsteps crunching through the snow, moving from the porch towards the driveway. The smell from earlier had intensified, seeping through the cracks in the cabin, pungent and overwhelming. Something, or someone, was prowling around our home. And they stank.

I scrambled out of bed, shaking Theo awake. It was around 3:30 AM, and he was groggy and disoriented, but the urgency in my voice snapped him to attention. I quickly relayed what had happened, my words tumbling out in a rush. Theo's face hardened with concern, and he immediately went to retrieve his 12-gauge shotgun from the closet.

I handed him the flashlight, the beam cutting through

the darkness as he cautiously stepped onto the back porch. The cold air hit us like a wall, the smell now almost unbearable. Theo shined the light around, and there they were—large, man-like footprints pressed into the snow, leading away from the porch.

"Elizabeth, get back inside," Theo whispered, his voice tight with fear. He followed me back into the cabin, slamming the door shut behind us. We stayed awake for the rest of the night, huddled together, every creak and whisper of the wind outside keeping us on edge.

When dawn finally broke, the world outside looked deceptively serene, the snow glistening under the pale morning sun. Despite our fear, we knew we had to investigate further. We bundled up and headed into town to buy film and plaster, determined to document what we had seen and make a cast of the footprints.

Back at the cabin, we carefully mixed the plaster, but in our haste, we made it too runny. As we poured it into what we thought was the best track, the plaster soaked through the snow, ruining the impression. Frustrated but undeterred, we made a thicker batch and poured it into the same track. This time, it held, but we soon realized we had no idea how to get the cast out without damaging it.

Not wanting to destroy the evidence, we decided to cover the tracks with cardboard boxes and wait until spring when the snow would melt and we could retrieve the casts more easily. It was a long, tense wait, filled with sleepless nights and nervous glances over our shoulders. The smell lingered around the cabin for days, a constant reminder of our mysterious visitor.

As the snow began to melt and the days grew longer, we finally felt ready to uncover the casts. Carefully, we lifted the cardboard boxes and found the plaster intact, though a bit weathered from the months of waiting. With great care, we managed to extract the casts from the now-softened ground. The detail was incredible—large, humanoid footprints, unlike anything we had ever seen.

We took photographs and contacted a local wildlife expert, hoping for some explanation. When he saw the casts and the photos, his expression turned serious. He couldn't definitively say what had made the prints, but he agreed they were highly unusual. He suggested sending the casts to a university for further analysis.

The months that followed were a blur of emails, phone calls, and mounting anticipation. The university's response was both exciting and frustrating. They confirmed that the footprints were not those of any known animal in the region, but beyond that, they couldn't provide a definitive answer. The possibility of a hoax was considered, but the remote location of our cabin and the circumstances of the encounter made that unlikely.

Our story began to spread, drawing interest from researchers, journalists, and even a few cryptozoologists. Some were skeptical, others fascinated, but none could offer a concrete explanation. The mystery of the footprints and the strange visitor in the night remained unresolved.

Every now and then, we would catch a whiff of that same odor or hear a distant rustling in the woods, and the fear would resurface. But as time passed, those moments became less frequent, and we learned to coexist with the fact that a large creature shared this land with us.

THE NIGHT ON THE GRAVEL ROAD

I'm familiar with the thick woods, foggy hills, and the twisting dirt roads that snake through the wild. Yet nothing could have prepared me for what I witnessed one night about 15 years ago. I'm Wendy and here's what happened.

It was late, probably around midnight. I was driving home from a friend's house, enjoying the quiet hum of my car against the gravel. The night was pitch black, the only light coming from my headlights cutting through the darkness. It was a cool night, and I had the windows down, letting the breeze fill the car.

As I navigated a particularly winding section of the

road, something caught my eye. A large, black, bipedal creature darted across the road ahead of me. I gasped and slammed on the brakes, skidding slightly on the loose gravel. The creature moved with incredible speed, but what struck me the most was the way it moved. It didn't run on two legs like a person or even on all fours like an animal. Instead, it moved on its feet and hands, almost like a grotesque, oversized spider.

As it crossed the road, it turned its head and looked directly at me. Our eyes met, and I have never felt terror like that before or since. Its face was something out of a nightmare—dark, leathery skin, with deep-set, glowing eyes that seemed to bore into my soul. The brief glimpse I got of its face is something I will never forget. It was as if time had slowed down in that moment, and I was frozen, unable to look away. I wish I had.

Then, as quickly as it had appeared, it vanished into the trees on the other side of the road. I sat there in stunned silence, my heart beating a million miles an hour. I wanted to believe it was just a trick of the light, maybe an animal I had never seen before. But deep down, I knew that wasn't true.

It wasn't long before strange things started happening around my home. I live in a secluded area, surrounded by dense woods. It's usually peaceful and quiet, but at night, the woods seemed to come alive with strange sounds.

Late at night, I would hear what sounded like hammering and screaming coming from the woods behind my house. The sounds were distant but unmistakable, a rhythmic pounding followed by high-pitched screams that sent shivers down my spine.

At first, I tried to ignore it, telling myself it was just my imagination or maybe some kind of animal. But as the nights went on, the sounds became more frequent and more intense. I would lie in bed, wide awake, listening to the eerie noises and feeling a growing sense of dread.

I started to talk to my neighbors, hoping someone else had heard the sounds or seen something unusual. Most of them dismissed my concerns, saying it was probably just wildlife or the sounds of the forest. But one elderly neighbor, Mrs. Henderson, took my questions seriously.

She told me stories about the area, tales of strange creatures and unexplained phenomena. She spoke of an old legend about a creature that lived in the woods, a beast that moved on its hands and feet and had a face that could freeze your blood. Her words made me shudder, and I realized that what I had seen might be connected to these old stories.

The screams and hammering sounds tapered off over the next couple of months. As time went on I became more comfortable at night but the fear of seeing that creature has never left me.

I am much more cautious of my surroundings now and have increased the security lights I have around my house. It gives me a little comfort, but not much.

THE SUMMER OF 1972

WASHINGTON

The summer of 1972 was one of those golden times in my life, filled with adventure and exploration. My cousin, Troy, and I were practically inseparable back then. We were both heading into the eighth grade, full of energy and curiosity. That summer, we planned a weekend fishing trip on the South Fork of the Nooksack River, a place that held the promise of both adventure and relaxation.

Our parents, trusting and perhaps a little crazy, dropped us off on a Friday afternoon at the end of Strand Road off Highway 9, between Sedro-Woolley and the Mount Baker Highway. They left us there with our camping gear, a few basic supplies, and instructions to be careful. They promised to pick us up on Sunday, and with that, they drove off, leaving us to our own devices.

We set up camp about 50 feet from the river, close to the end of the road. It was a beautiful spot, surrounded by dense forest and the gentle murmur of the river. We spent the afternoon fishing, enjoying the peace and the thrill of catching our own dinner. As the sun began to set, we returned to our camp, built a fire, and cooked our catch. The evening was filled with laughter and stories, the kind of carefree fun that only comes from being young and free.

After our meal, we settled into our sleeping bags, exhausted but happy. We each stuck our pocket knives in the sand next to us, a precaution that seemed both practical and a little thrilling. I remember falling asleep to the crackling of the fire and the sound of the river, feeling perfectly content.

But sometime in the middle of the night, I was startled awake by a sound. It was a soft, hissing noise that seemed out of place in the stillness of the night. As I lay there in my sleeping bag, my heart pounding, I saw the silhouette of something on the other side of a small fence, just slightly above us. The full moon behind it created a perfect, haunting image.

The creature was no more than 20 feet away, its upper body clearly visible in the moonlight. It was broad-shouldered with no neck, a sloping forehead, and no noticeable ears. It made a series of long hissing sounds, that freaked me the hell out. It would hiss, pause, and then hiss again, repeating this five or six times.

The silhouette was terrifying. It rocked slightly from side to side, as if it was trying to see us better or maybe smell us. It appeared to be crouching, perhaps on one knee, as it couldn't get any closer without going through the fence and under some small branches. I was petrified, unable to move or make a sound. I just lay there, watching, my body stiff with fear.

The creature stayed there for what felt like an hour, but was probably only three to five minutes. When it finally left, it pivoted its entire body to the right and disappeared into the darkness. I heard nothing as it walked away, no sound of footsteps or rustling leaves. I just lay there, too scared to move, my body cramping up from the tension.

Shortly after it left, I heard a series of clicks and what sounded like rocks being hit together rapidly. The sounds came from the direction of the river, across from where we were. They were hit together three to five times very fast, and I heard this a few times, first close by, then farther away, as if the creature was moving away from us.

My cousin Troy slept through the whole thing. I didn't wake him, partly because I was too scared to move and partly because I wasn't sure what to say. The next morning, as the sun began to rise, I finally felt safe enough to move. I shook Troy awake and told him everything. He listened, wide-eyed, but skeptical. We spent the morning looking for tracks, but the field where the creature had been was hard-packed and dry, leaving no indentations.

We stayed another night, though I was far from comfortable. We built a big fire and tied fishing line to each other's wrists, a makeshift alarm system in case something happened. But the night passed without incident, and by Sunday, our parents arrived to pick us up, none the wiser about the terror I had experienced.

I found it difficult to let go of that memory. That fear. I knew what I had seen was not a man, not a bear, and not someone playing a prank.

Years went by, and I kept the experience mostly to myself. It was hard to explain, and even harder to get people to believe me. But I knew what I had seen, and the fear was real. Even now, nearly 52 years later, the memory is as vivid as ever.

4TH OF JULY ENCOUNTER

My name is Samantha and this story happened a long time ago, during the summer of 1978. It was the 4th of July weekend, and I was driving home late after visiting my mother. My baby girl was asleep in the back seat, and I was just trying to get us home safely. I had no idea that drive would turn into the most terrifying experience of my life.

The night was dark and quiet as I navigated the winding, gravel roads. I was driving cautiously, going about 35 mph, when I approached a corner with a guardrail to my right. Below the guardrail was a gully with a creek at the bottom, and a telephone pole about three feet from the end of the guardrail.

As I rounded the corner, my headlights began to illuminate something ahead. At first, I thought it was just a telephone pole or part of the guardrail. But as I got closer, I realized it was something crouched down on the last cement guardrail post. I felt my heart beat quicken as I tried to make sense of what I was seeing.

When I got closer, the thing stood up from its crouching position, almost as if it had been sitting on its heels. It leaped into the middle of my lane and threw its hands up in the air, trying to make itself look bigger. In that instant, my headlights fully illuminated it, and I got a clear look at the creature.

It was about seven feet tall, not much bigger than my stepdad and brothers who are around 6'2" to 6'4". It was all black and definitely not a bear. I've seen black bears before, and this was nothing like that. Its arms stretched high like a man's, not like a bear's, and its face was more human-like, without the longer nose of a bear. It had a flat face, almost like a man, not a dog.

The creature seemed as shocked as I was, and in a split second, it realized I wasn't going to stop. It dropped to the ground right in front of my car. I had no time to react. My little Honda Civic sedan went right over it with a loud boom-boom as all four tires ran over its body. The impact jolted me, and I gripped the steering wheel, my heart pounding.

My mind was racing. I thought about stopping to check if it was still alive, but fear took over. What if it came after me? What if it had damaged my car and I got stuck out there with it and my baby girl? I couldn't risk it. I cried the whole way home, terrified and convinced that I had just killed the only Bigfoot in existence.

When I finally got home, I found a note from my family saying they had gone up to Canada to visit a wave pool and wouldn't be back until later. There was no way to contact them. I put my daughter to bed and sat down, trying to figure out what to do. After about half an hour, I decided to call 911. I told them I had hit a bear and was worried it might be injured and pose a threat to the children living down a private driveway nearby. I also mentioned that if it was dead, it could cause an accident since it was in the road.

As soon as I got off the phone with 911, I went out to check the damage to my car. Amazingly, there was very little as I expected all underneath the car to be ripped out. The only thing I noticed was that my license plate holder with the dealership's name was broken in half, and the bottom half was missing. The license plate itself was bent under the car. I bent it back and saw some hair hanging from the license plate bolt.

My dogs were circling the car, sniffing and whining. They wouldn't leave it alone. I grabbed the hair, thinking maybe I should keep it, but in my panic, I threw it into the garbage. The hair was dark brown with reddish highlights and felt wiry. Later, I would regret not keeping it, especially when DNA testing became more accessible.

When my family got home, I told them what happened. My brothers teased me, and my parents were skeptical. To prove I wasn't crazy, I called 911 the next day to check on my report. To my shock, they had no record of my call. Even after I gave them the exact time, they couldn't find it.

Determined to prove myself, I took one of my brothers back to the spot where I had hit the creature. I expected to find some evidence—hair, blood, or at least the other half of my license plate holder—but there was nothing. The road was clean, as if nothing had happened. My brother thought I was insane.

Over the years, I've only told a few close friends and family about the encounter. Most of them think it's a joke or a figment of my imagination. But I know what I saw. The creature was real, and the experience was terrifying.

Sometimes, late at night, I hear a cry that can only be described as a Bigfoot's howl. It's a haunting sound that brings back all the fear and confusion from that night. But I've never seen another one, and I don't expect to. The encounter remains a mystery, one that has stay with me for decades.

The only reason I'm coming forward now is that I recently learned about organizations that investigate Bigfoot sightings. I want my brothers to apologize for teasing me all these years, though I won't hold my breath. I hope that by sharing my story, others who have had similar experiences will feel validated.

BIGFOOT AT THE GAS STATION

OREGON

Our small town, nestled between dense forests and fog-covered mountains, has always been a place of peace and serenity for me. While closing up the gas station where I worked, that peace was shattered and I haven't been the same since.

I was working the night shift at the old gas station off Route 2, a job I took to help pay for college. The hours were long and the nights quiet, but it was usually an easy gig. I'd finish my homework, listen to music, and occasionally chat with the few late-night customers who stopped by. That night started out no different, but it ended in a way I could have never imagined.

It was late, around midnight, when I began my closing

routine. I had just finished cleaning the counters and was counting the cash drawer when I noticed the lights flickering slightly. It wasn't unusual; the station was old, and the wiring had always been a bit faulty. I didn't think much of it and continued with my work.

After I finished with the cash drawer, I went outside to lock the pumps. The night was silent, the only sound was the faint breeze through the trees. The station was surrounded by thick woods on three sides, with the highway stretching out in front. It suddenly felt darker, the trees casting long, shadowy fingers across the ground.

As I was locking the last pump, I felt goosebumps spread across my arms and legs. It wasn't from the cool air; it was a deep, primal fear. I turned around slowly, my eyes scanning the tree line and there it was.

Just beyond the reach of the station's lights, a dark humanoid figure stood motionless. My first thought was that it was a person, maybe a vagrant or someone lost. But as my eyes adjusted, I realized this was no human. The figure was tall, much taller than anyone I had ever seen. It was covered in dark hair, blending almost seamlessly with the shadows of the trees. I think the only reason I could see it was because it seemed to absorb the light in its thick black coat.

I stood still, my heart hammering away in my chest. The creature didn't move, and for a moment, I thought maybe my eyes were playing tricks on me. But then it stepped forward, just enough for the dim light to catch its face. It had a broad, flat nose and deep-set eyes that glowed red. Its mouth was slightly open, revealing sharp teeth that sent a jolt of fear through me.

I stumbled backward, nearly tripping over my own feet. I fumbled with the lock on the pump, my hands shaking uncontrollably. The creature watched me, its gaze never wavering. It took another step forward, and I could see its massive hands, each finger ending in a sharp, claw-like nail.

Somehow, I managed to lock the pump and sprinted back to the station. I slammed the door shut and locked it, gasping for breath. I pressed my back against the door, trying to calm my racing heart. For a moment, I considered calling the police, but what would I say? That I saw a monster outside the gas station? They'd think I was crazy.

I cautiously peered out the window, my eyes searching the darkness for any sign of the creature. At first, I saw nothing, but then a shadow shifted near the edge of the forest. It was still there, watching me. I grabbed the phone and dialed my boss's number, hoping he might have some advice on what to do. The phone rang and rang, but there was no answer. I was on my own.

The minutes ticked by slowly. I kept glancing at the window, expecting to see the creature come closer, but it stayed just outside the circle of light, lurking in the shadows. I felt trapped, the station suddenly feeling like a cage. Every creak and groan of the building made me jump, my nerves frayed to the breaking point.

Finally, after what felt like hours, I saw the creature move again. It stepped fully into the light this time, and I got a good look at it. It was even more terrifying up close. It stood well over seven feet tall, its body covered in thick, black and gray fur. Its eyes glowed faintly in the dim light, and its mouth was twisted into a snarl.

It moved slowly, deliberately, towards the station. I backed away from the window, my heart pounding in my ears. I needed to do something, but my mind was blank with fear. The creature reached the edge of the pavement and stopped, staring at the station, at me.

Without thinking, I grabbed the nearest thing I could find—a heavy flashlight—and held it up defensively. The creature tilted its head slightly, as if curious. Then, to my utter horror, it let out a low growl and took another step forward.

Instinct took over. I bolted for the back room, slamming the door behind me. I searched frantically for anything I could use as a weapon, my hands shaking uncontrollably. I found an old metal pipe and gripped it tightly, my knuckles white.

The back room had a small window, and I peered out, hoping to see if the creature had followed. To my relief, it was still standing by the edge of the pavement, watching the front of the station. I knew I couldn't stay hidden forever, but the thought of confronting that thing made feel nauseous.

I took a deep breath and tried to think rationally. The creature hadn't tried to break in yet, which meant it was either cautious or not particularly aggressive. Maybe I could scare it off. I glanced around the back room and spotted an old air horn. It wasn't much, but it was loud. Maybe loud enough to startle the creature and buy me some time.

I grabbed the air horn and the metal pipe, steeling myself for what I had to do. Slowly, I crept back to the front of the station, keeping to the shadows. The creature was still there, its eyes fixed on the building.

With my heart in my throat, I stepped out into the open and pressed the button on the air horn. The blaring sound shattered the silence, echoing through the night. The creature flinched, its head snapping in my direction. For a moment, I thought it might flee, but then it let out an earsplitting roar and stepped back.

Panic overwhelmed me, and I stumbled backward, dropping the air horn. The creature continued to stare at me, its eyes full of curiosity rather than rage. It was almost as if it was trying to understand me, to gauge whether I was a threat.

For a tense moment, we stared at each other. My fear was still there, but I could see something in its eyes that I hadn't noticed before—a hint of intelligence, of awareness. It wasn't just a mindless beast; it was something more.

Slowly, I lowered the metal pipe, trying to show that I wasn't a threat. The creature watched me, its eyes flicking between the pipe and my face. Then, to my surprise, it took a step back, retreating slightly into the shadows.

I stood there, still, as the creature turned and walked away, disappearing into the forest. I didn't move until I was sure it was gone, the silence of the night enveloping me once again. My hands were still shaking, and I felt a wave of relief and confusion wash over me.

I knew I had just experienced something extraordinary, something that defied explanation. I don't think my brain could process exactly what my eyes had seen.

I shared my story with some of my family members. Most were skeptical, while a few were intrigued. My boss at the gas station listened with wide eyes but ultimately decided to increase security around the station, just in case.

To anyone reading this, I encourage you to embrace the unknown. Keep your eyes and ears open, stay curious, and never stop searching for the wonders that make life so extraordinary. The world is a vast and wondrous place, filled with secrets waiting to be discovered. And sometimes, the most extraordinary stories are the ones we least expect.

WEREWOLF FROM THOSE UNDERWORLD MOVIES

ILLINOIS

My name is Lydia, I am forty-seven years old and here is my encounter story.

It was a cool autumn evening with the air carrying the scent of fallen leaves. I had just finished dinner and decided to take my little dog, Max, out for his nightly potty break. Max is a small terrier mix, full of energy and always eager for a walk. I clipped on his leash and stepped out onto the porch, letting him sniff around the yard.

I stood on the porch, enjoying the quiet of the evening. The street was mostly deserted, with only a few houses dotting the landscape. The streetlights cast a soft glow, creating long shadows that danced with the breeze. Max was busy exploring a particularly interesting patch of grass when I noticed something way down the street.

At first, it was just a flicker of movement, something I could have easily dismissed as an animal or a neighbor. But as I focused, I felt a sudden and inexplicable sense of dread. My heart began to race, and I instinctively tightened my grip on Max's leash. He looked up at me, sensing my unease.

The movement became clearer, and I could make out a shape—a dark, hulking figure moving between the trees three blocks away. I couldn't fathom what I was seeing. It didn't make sense in the real world. I knew I had to get Max and myself back inside, away from whatever it was.

I called to Max, trying to keep my voice steady. "Come on, Max, let's go inside." He seemed reluctant to leave his spot, but I tugged gently on his leash, and he trotted over to me. As I turned to head back to the house, I couldn't resist glancing over my shoulder.

What I saw made my legs go weak. The creature had emerged from the trees and was now standing in the middle of the street, only two blocks away. It was massive, I'd say seven feet tall, with wide shoulders and a tapered chest, like a v-shape. Its legs were thin but even from that distance I could tell this creature was well muscled. What struck me the most was its face—it looked like something straight out of a nightmare, like a werewolf from those Underworld movies. *How was this happening*, I thought.

The creature began to move towards us, its gait slow and purposeful. Panic gripped me, and I scooped up Max, clutching him tightly to my chest. I ran up the porch steps and fumbled with the door, my hands shaking uncontrollably. I managed to get the door open and rushed inside, slamming it shut behind me.

I locked the door and bolted it, my heart pounding so loudly I could barely hear anything else. I cautiously peered through the window, trying to see if the creature had followed us. The street was empty, but the sense of dread lingered. I backed away from the window, still holding Max, and collapsed onto the couch.

For the next few hours, I sat in fear, my thoughts swirling with fear and confusion. I kept all the lights off, not wanting to draw any attention. Every slight noise made me jump. Max seemed to sense my fear and stayed close to me, his small body trembling and he nudged his head behind my back.

I couldn't get the image of the creature out of my mind. Its eyes, its fur, the way it moved—it was all so vivid, so real. I had never believed in werewolves or any kind of supernatural creatures, but what I saw that night defied explanation.

Eventually, exhaustion took over, and I dozed off on the couch with Max in my arms. When I woke up, it was morning, and the first rays of sunlight were streaming through the windows. I felt a sense of relief, but the fear from the night before still clung to me.

I tried to go about my day as normally as possible, but it was hard to get that image out of my head. The events of the previous night played over and over in my mind, and I found myself constantly looking around for this thing. I avoided going out after dark, and when I had to, I made sure I wasn't alone.

I found myself replaying every detail in my mind, trying to piece together an accurate description.

The creature had a powerful, muscular build, with long, sinewy limbs. Its hands were large, with sharp, claw-like nails that gleamed in the dim light. Its fur was dark, almost black, and looked coarse and somewhat matted. But it was the face that haunted me the most. It had a pronounced snout, with sharp teeth that were visible even from a distance. Its eyes glowed with an eerie, yellowish light, and there was an intelligence in them that made me feel very uneasy.

It made me feel like it knew what I was thinking and that it enjoyed terrorizing me.

I found it incredibly hard to put the sighting behind me. It was hard to go outside at night, even just to take Max out for a quick potty break. I installed extra locks on my doors and made sure all the windows were securely fastened. I even considered getting a larger dog for added protection, but I knew that no animal or locks for that matter, could protect me from what I had seen.

I avoided talking about the encounter, fearing that people would think I was crazy.

As I sit here now eight years later, writing down my story, I still feel anxiety about that night. I hope I never see anything like it ever again.

Thank you for taking the time to read my encounter.

THE CREATURE BY THE LAKE

My name is Maureen and I've lived in a rural setting my whole life and couldn't imagine being stuck in a concrete jungle. There's something about living near water that has always soothed me and made me feel at peace.

I live in a two-story house overlooking a small lake with neighbors either side. There's a road that runs between my house and the water, but it's usually quiet, especially late at night. My bedroom is at the front of the house, with a large window that gives me a perfect view of the lake. It's my favorite spot to sit and relax, watching the water ripple and the trees sway in the breeze. But, that window fills me with a sense of dread now.

It was a warm summer night, and I had gone to bed early after a long day at work. Around 2 AM, I woke up suddenly. I don't know why, but something compelled me to get up and look out the window. Maybe it was a noise, or maybe it was just a feeling, but I couldn't ignore it.

I crept out of bed and moved slowly to the window, careful not to make a sound. The house was silent, and the only light came from the moon reflecting off the lake. As I looked out, my eyes were drawn to a large, dark shape on the grass near the water. At first, I thought it was just a large rock like a boulder, but something about it seemed off. I didn't remember a boulder being there before.

I stared at it, my heart beginning to pound in my chest. Then I saw a small movement, just enough to catch my eye. I realized with a shock that it wasn't a rock at all. It was an animal, crouching low to the ground. My breath caught in my throat as I noticed an ear twitching, as if it was listening.

As I continued to watch, the animal lifted its head slightly, and I saw its long snout. It looked like a wolf, but it was too large and its fur was patchy. It kind of reminded me of a hyena. It gave me the creeps looking all sinister. Anxiety coursed through my veins and I was unable to tear my eyes away.

The creature remained perfectly still, waiting. Then, a lone car drove down the road, its headlights cutting through the darkness. As soon as the car passed, the creature sprang into action, running on all fours after it. It moved with incredible speed, disappearing where I couldn't see it anymore.

I stood there trying to rationalize what it was. What had I just seen? My logical mind tried to come up with explanations—maybe it was just a sickly dog, or a coyote. But deep down, I knew it was something else, something that shouldn't belong here.

I finally forced myself to move, stepping back from the window and sitting down on the edge of my bed. I tried to calm myself down, telling myself it was just an animal, nothing more. But the image of that creature, with its long snout and mangy fur, wouldn't go away.

There was no way I could go back to sleep. I spent the rest of the night sitting by the window, staring out at the lake and the road, hoping and dreading to see the creature again. But it didn't come back, and as the first light of dawn began to break, I finally felt a small sense of relief.

I moved soon after that sighting to a few counties over after, having moved in with my now fiance. I haven't told a soul what I saw that night, other than submitting my story to you. I didn't want people asking questions about it as I have tried to block that vision from my mind. It is best left in the past.

THE DISAPPEARANCE

OHIO

I grew up in a small town in Ohio during the 1990s. My best friend, Ben, and I were inseparable. We did everything together—from riding bikes around the neighborhood to fishing in the creek behind his house. Ben lived on a semi-rural farm on the outskirts of town, a place surrounded by woods and open fields. We spent countless hours exploring those woods, building forts, and pretending to be adventurers. Those were the golden days of my youth, but they were also the days that will stick with me forever.

It was late September when Ben went missing. We had just started eighth grade, and life was as normal as it could be for a couple of teenage boys. One Friday afternoon,

Ben didn't show up at school. At first, I thought he might be sick, but when I called his house, there was no answer. My concern grew when I rode my bike over to his place and found his mom pacing frantically in the driveway. She explained that Ben had gone out to the woods the previous evening and hadn't come back. They had already searched the surrounding area and called the Sheriff, but there was no sign of him. The whole town rallied together, forming search parties and scouring the woods day and night. But as days turned into weeks, hope began to fade. Ben was never found and I was devastated.

In the days following Ben's disappearance, whispers and rumors spread through the town like wildfire. People talked about the Ohio Grassman, a local legend akin to Bigfoot. According to the stories, the Grassman was a large, ape-like creature that roamed the woods of Ohio. Some claimed to have seen it; others dismissed it as mere folklore. But after Ben vanished, the tales took on a new, eerie significance.

I had heard these stories growing up, but I never took them seriously. To me, they were just part of the local lore, something to scare kids from staying out too late. But now, with Ben gone, I couldn't help but wonder if there was some truth to them.

Two weeks after Ben's disappearance, I had my own encounter that changed everything. It was a Saturday afternoon, and I was out in the woods behind Ben's house, hoping to find some clue, some trace of my friend. The sky was overcast, and a light drizzle fell, making the forest feel even more somber and foreboding.

I was about a mile in when I noticed a strange stillness in the air. The usual sounds of birds and rustling leaves were absent, replaced by an oppressive silence. My father had told me that when the woods go silent it meant there was a predator around so I decided it was time to head back.

As I turned, I look over to my right and saw an unusual shape. At first, I thought it was a tree or a stump, but as I focused, I realized it was moving. A massive, dark figure stood about fifty yards away, partially hidden by the trees. I couldn't make sense of what I was seeing and I wanted to look away but I couldn't.

It was tall, like a basketball player tall, with auburn-red hair that hung about six inches long. Its arms were long and muscular, and its upper body was thick with muscles. I don't remember if it had a neck, but I do recall thinking that its head seemed too small for its body. And boy did it stink. A mix of feces, a dead animal and rotting meat wafted over to me and I nearly gagged.

It turned its head and looked directly at me with massive, black, intelligent eyes. For a moment, we locked gazes, and I felt a wave of fear and awe wash over me. Then, it simply reached over and put its arm onto a tree and walked past it and into the forest.

I ran back to Ben's house as fast as I could, my mind utterly jumbled with confusion. I knew what I had seen wasn't normal. It wasn't a bear or any other animal I'd ever encountered. It was something else, something out of the stories we had heard all our lives. To me it looked like a monster.

Ben's parents weren't home so I ran down the road to my house.

When I got home, I told my parents what I had seen. They listened but were skeptical. My dad suggested it was just my imagination, heightened by the stress of losing my friend. But deep down, I knew it was real. I knew the Ohio Grassman was real, and I was convinced it had something to do with Ben's disappearance.

As the weeks went by, the search for Ben continued, but with no leads and no new evidence, it eventually dwindled. Life in our small town returned to a semblance of normalcy, but for me, nothing was the same. I couldn't forget what I had seen. It haunted my dreams, and I would wake in a cold sweat.

As the years passed, I learned to live with the uncertainty. The pain of losing Ben never went away, but I found ways to cope.

I still live in Ohio, not far from where I grew up. The woods that once filled me with fear now bring a sense of peace. I've come to accept that some questions may never be answered, and that's okay. Life is full of mysteries, and sometimes the journey is more important than the destination.

THE LONG WALK HOME

MAINE

Growing up in a small town where everyone knows each other has its perks. The luscious forests and open fields are like a playground for kids, but they can also hide secrets and shadows. This story takes place when I was 17 years old, and it's a memory that still makes me shiver. Now, at 32, I've never forgotten that night.

It was a brisk autumn evening, and I had spent the evening at my friend Silas's house, hanging out and playing video games. Time flew by, and before I knew it, it was almost midnight. Silas's house was only two miles from mine, a walk I had done countless times, so I wasn't worried about heading home late.

I said goodbye to Silas and stepped out into the night.

The sky was clear, and the moon was nearly full, allowing me to see the landscape pretty well. The walk home took me along a quiet road that bordered a large cornfield, and the tall stalks rustled softly in the gentle breeze. I stuffed my hands into my jacket pockets and started walking, my footsteps echoing in the stillness.

About halfway home, I began to notice a faint noise in the cornfield to my left. At first, I thought it was just the wind, but the sound seemed rhythmic. I stopped for a moment, straining to hear over the pounding of my heart. The sound stopped too. I shook my head, trying to brush off the uneasy feeling that was creeping over me, and continued walking.

After a few more steps, I heard it again. This time, it was closer, and it sounded like something was pacing me, matching my steps. My heart started beating faster, and I quickened my pace. The rustling quickened too. I could hear the stalks snapping and parting as something large moved through the field, but I couldn't see anything. The corn was too tall and dense.

The sound was unmistakable now—whatever or whoever it was, it was walking on two legs. The deliberate, heavy footsteps echoed my own, sending a surge of adrenaline through my body. I fought the urge to break into a run, knowing that if I did, I might provoke whatever was out there.

I glanced around, hoping to see a glimpse of something,

anything, that could explain the noise. But the moonlight, while bright, cast too many shadows, and the cornfield remained an impenetrable wall of darkness. I forced myself to keep a steady pace, my eyes darting back and forth, ears straining to catch every sound.

Fear started to grip me like a vice. Every step felt like an eternity, and the road ahead seemed to stretch on forever. I could hear the creature's breaths now, heavy and labored, mirroring my own growing panic. My mind raced with possibilities—was it a bear? But bears don't walk on two legs. A prankster? But no one could move so swiftly and silently through the corn.

I was about half a mile from home when the creature let out a deep growl that lasted around twenty seconds. The sound was so deep it vibrated through my chest. I knew then that this was no ordinary animal. Every instinct screamed at me to run, but I forced myself to stay calm, to keep walking. It wasn't easy.

The final stretch of the walk felt like a nightmare. The creature never showed itself, but I could feel its presence, its eyes on me, tracking my every move. The road was empty, and the only sound was the relentless rustling of the corn and the thud of my heartbeat in my ears.

I could see the lights of my trailer in the distance, a beacon of safety. I focused on those lights, willing myself to reach them. The growling stopped, but the rustling continued, always just out of sight. I was so close, just a few hundred yards away.

Then the rustling stopped. The abrupt silence was more terrifying than the noise. I knew it was now or never. I broke into a sprint, my feet pounding the pavement as I raced towards home. I didn't dare look back, didn't want to see what might be chasing me.

I burst through the front door, slamming it shut behind me and locking it. I stood there, panting and trembling, trying to get myself under control. My parents were already in bed, and my mom yelled out not to slam the door. I made my way to my room, confused and utterly freaked out.

I barely slept that night. Every sound outside my window made me jump, my imagination running wild.

The next morning, I told my parents what had happened. They listened, concerned but skeptical. My dad suggested it was just a deer or maybe a stray dog. But I knew what I had heard, the heavy footsteps, the growl—it was no natural animal.

For weeks, I avoided walking home alone at night. I couldn't shake the fear that had taken hold of me. Even during the day, I found myself glancing nervously at the cornfield whenever I passed it.

Over time, I developed my own theories about what had happened. Maybe it was an animal, something big and unusual for the area. Or perhaps it was a person, someone playing a cruel joke. But deep down, I knew it was something more, something that I am glad I never saw.

THE CHASE

My husband Miguel and I are North Carolina born and bred. We've always loved the outdoors, and funnily enough we met on a hiking trip, and it seemed fitting that we spent most of our time together exploring the trails and mountains of our beautiful state. This story takes place a few months after our wedding, during a hike that started out like any other.

It was a perfect autumn day, the kind that makes you want to be outside, soaking up the fresh air and vibrant colors of the changing leaves. Miguel and I decided to hike a popular trail that led to an overlook with a breathtaking view of the valley below. We packed a lunch, filled our water bottles, and set off, eager for a day of adventure.

The trail was moderately difficult, winding through dense forest before opening up to the overlook. We encountered a few other hikers along the way, exchanging friendly nods and smiles. The sun filtered through the trees, casting dappled shadows on the path, and the scent of pine and earth filled the air. It was the kind of day that made you feel alive and grateful for the beauty of nature.

We reached the overlook just before noon. The view was spectacular, the valley stretching out below us like a vast, colorful tapestry. We sat on a large rock, unpacked our lunch, and enjoyed the peaceful silence. As we ate, we talked about our plans for the future, our dreams and aspirations. It was one of those perfect moments that you wish could last forever.

After we finished eating, we sat in comfortable silence, taking in the view. That's when I saw it. At first, I thought it was just a large dog or maybe a coyote, running through the valley below. But as I watched, I realized it was much larger than any dog I had ever seen. It moved with incredible speed and grace, covering the ground effortlessly on all fours.

Miguel and I watched in fascinated silence as the creature continued to run through the valley. It was dark, but had patches of gray, and its movements were fluid and powerful. But then it did something that I didn't expect. It stopped, lifted its head, and sniffed the air. For a moment, it seemed to be searching for something. Then, to our horror, it stood up on its hind legs. Seeing that instantly made me feel queasy. It didn't look natural.

The creature was enormous, even from this distance. Its body was muscular and covered in dark hair or fur, and its head was that of a dog or wolf, with sharp, pointed ears and a long snout. The hair around its head was long, like a lion's mane. It turned its head in our direction, and even from that distance, I could feel its eyes on us. My heart leapt into my throat as I realized that this was no ordinary animal.

As if it had heard us, the creature bared its lips and began to move in our direction. At first, it walked slowly, but then it dropped back down on all fours and started to run. Panic gripped me, and I grabbed Miguel's arm.

We took off down the trail, our hearts pounding and our breaths coming fast and hard. After about a mile, I could hear the creature behind us, its powerful limbs crashing through the underbrush. I didn't dare look back, knowing that the sight would only fuel my terror. We passed other hikers along the way, shouting that there was a bear in the area, hoping they would turn around and head back to safety.

The trail seemed to stretch on forever, the trees blurring into a dizzying tunnel of green and brown. My legs burned with effort, and my lungs felt like they were on fire, but I didn't stop. I couldn't stop. I was absolutely petrified.

Thankfully, we finally burst out of the forest and into the parking lot. Our car was in sight, and I felt a surge of relief. We sprinted the last few yards, fumbling with the keys in our panic. Miguel managed to unlock the doors, and we scrambled inside, slamming the doors shut behind us.

I locked the doors and looked around, expecting to see the creature burst out of the trees at any moment. But there was nothing. The parking lot was eerily silent, the only sound our ragged breathing and the thud of our racing hearts.

Miguel started the car, and we sped out of the parking lot, not daring to look back. We didn't stop until we were miles away, the safety of civilization finally calming our frantic nerves. Only then did we begin to process what had happened.

We spent the rest of the drive home in stunned silence, each lost in our own thoughts. The creature we had seen defied explanation, and the terror we had felt was something I had never experienced before. It wasn't until we were safely back in our apartment that we finally talked about it.

The experience left us both shaken. We avoided hiking for a while, the memory of that day too fresh and too terrifying. When we finally did venture back out, we were much more cautious, always on the lookout for any signs of danger. The joy and peace we had once found in nature were now tainted by fear and uncertainty.

Even now, years later, the memory of that day is vivid in my mind. The sight of the creature and the sheer terror of the chase is something I'll never forget.

THE BOOGER THAT TOOK MY FATHER

ALABAMA

Our family homestead, nestled in the semi-rural outskirts of Birmingham, was my world. It was a place of rolling rich pastures, thick woods, and wide-open skies—a place where my father taught me to respect the land and the creatures that lived on it. This story takes place 27 years ago, when I was 13, and it's a memory that still haunts me to this day. I'm 40 now, and the events that unfolded back then changed my life forever.

It started with little things, the kind of odd occurrences you'd easily dismiss if they happened on their own. But together, they painted a picture of something sinister. One evening, I was sitting in the living room doing my homework when I heard a strange noise on the roof. It sounded like something heavy was moving around up there. At first, I thought it was a raccoon or maybe a stray cat, but the noise was way too loud.

My dad, always the protector, grabbed his shotgun and went outside to investigate. I followed him to the porch, curious about what could be up there. He circled the house, shining his flashlight up at the roof, but he didn't see anything. He told me to go back inside, but I could see the worry etched on his face.

That night was the beginning of a series of strange and frightening events that would escalate over the coming months. Our animals started disappearing—first a few chickens, then a goat. We found traces of blood, but no sign of the missing animals. My dad started carrying his shotgun everywhere, even when he was just walking from the house to the barn. His usual calm demeanor was replaced by a tense, watchful vigilance.

One evening, my dad and I were out in the paddock, fixing a broken fence. The sun was setting across the field. I was holding the flashlight while my dad hammered the last nail into place when we heard a long, low growl coming from the woods. My dad froze, his hand tightening on the hammer. He motioned for me to be quiet, and we listened.

The growl came again, closer this time. It was a deep, rough sound that instantly sent fear through my body. My dad handed me the hammer and picked up his shotgun, scanning the tree line with narrowed eyes. For a moment, everything was still. Then, we heard the sound of something moving through the underbrush, heavy footsteps that shook the ground.

"Billy, get back to the house," my dad said, his voice low and urgent.

I didn't argue. I ran back to the house as fast as my legs would carry me, the flashlight beam bouncing wildly in the darkness. I burst through the door, breathless and scared. My mom looked up from her knitting, alarmed.

"Something's out there," I said, my voice trembling. "Dad's got his shotgun."

From that night on, my dad's behavior changed even more. He was always on edge, always looking over his shoulder. He started setting traps around the property, and he installed extra locks on the doors and windows. I could see the strain in his eyes, the fear he tried to hide from us.

One night, I woke up to the sound of something scratching at my bedroom window. I lay there, frozen with fear, listening to the noise. It was a slow scratching, like claws scraping against the glass. I wanted to call out for my dad, but my voice seemed stuck in my throat.

Eventually, the scratching stopped, and I heard heavy footsteps walking away. I lay there, trembling, until the first light of dawn crept through the curtains. I ran downstairs to find my dad already up, his shotgun resting against the kitchen table.

"Something was at my window last night," I said, my voice barely above a whisper.

My dad's face tightened, and he nodded. "I know. I heard it too."

The tension in our home was thick, a constant undercurrent of fear and uncertainty. My dad tried to put on a brave face, but I could see the toll it was taking on him. He was losing weight, and there were dark circles under his eyes from lack of sleep.

Then, one day, he didn't come home.

He had gone out to the paddock to check on the animals and never returned. My mom and I waited, the hours stretching into an agonizing eternity. As darkness fell, we called the neighbors and the Sheriff. A search party was organized, and we combed the fields and woods, calling his name, but there was no sign of him.

His truck was still parked by the barn, and his shotgun lay on the ground near the tree line, bent out of shape as if it had been twisted by something with immense strength. But my dad was gone. The only clue was a trail of blood leading into the woods, but it eventually disappeared, leaving us with more questions than answers.

My dad's disappearance shattered our family. My mom was a wreck, and I felt like my world had been ripped apart.

The search continued for weeks, but hope began to fade. People started to whisper about the booger, a local legend of a creature that roamed the woods, preying on livestock and sometimes even people.

I had heard the stories before, but I never believed them. But growing up in Alabama, you learn to respect the land and the mysteries it holds. The dense woods and sprawling fields are beautiful, but they can also be unforgiving. My dad used to tell me that the land has a life of its own, that it watches over us but also demands respect. I never fully understood what he meant until those strange occurrences began.

As the months dragged on, it became clear that we couldn't stay on the farm. My mom couldn't handle the constant fear and grief, and we were struggling to make ends meet without my dad's income. The memories of those nights, the sounds, and the terror were too much to bear.

We sold the farm and moved into a small house in town. It was a difficult decision, but it was the only one that made sense. Leaving the farm felt like leaving a part of ourselves behind, but it also brought a sense of relief. The weight of the fear and the constant vigilance lifted, even if just a little.

Life has moved on and I have missed my father every day since. Mom has since passed on and I don't think she ever got over the shock of losing my father.

I have long since moved closer to the city with my family and feel much safer living with neighbors on either side of me.

THE NIGHT I HIT A BIGFOOT

I am Ray and I have spent over two decades as a state trooper, patrolling the highways and back roads of our state. Now retired, I spend my days hunting, fishing, and enjoying the tranquility of the Alabama wilderness. I thought I had seen it all—but I was very wrong.

It was a chilly November evening, I had been out hunting all day and decided to call it a night around sunset. I packed up my gear, loaded my truck, and began the drive home. My mind wandered to the upcoming Thanksgiving holiday and the time I'd spend with family.

Late-night drives on rural Alabama highways are usually serene, the roads often deserted at that hour. The steady drone of the engine and the consistent beat of tires on the pavement brought a kind of serenity I relished after a long day. However, I was unaware that this peacefulness was on the brink of being violently disrupted.

I was about an hour from home, driving along a stretch of highway that cut through dense forest on either side. The moonlight cast shadows on the road, but visibility was good. I rounded a bend when suddenly, something massive darted out from the trees and into my path. I had no time to react. There was a sickening thud as I clipped the creature with the front corner of my cruiser.

My heart pounded as I sat there, gripping the steering wheel. The front corner of my cruiser was crumpled. I fumbled for my flashlight, my hands trembling, and stepped out into the cold night air. The headlights illuminated a creature lying on the road.

This creature was enormous, even lying down it must have spanned at least seven or eight feet. Its body was cloaked in thick, dark brown, matted hair not fur, about three inches long. It had a vaguely human shape, but its features were distorted, resembling those of a great ape. There was no neck—the trapezius muscles were too thick to allow for one. Its hair was sparse on its face but thick everywhere else. Its eyes were shut, and it exhaled heavily, producing a deep, raspy noise that gave me the creeps.

I stood there, flashlight in one hand, my hunting rifle in the other, unsure of what to do. The logical part of my brain tried to rationalize what I was seeing, but nothing made sense. I had spent my career encountering all sorts of wild animals, but this didn't fit. It wasn't supposed to exist.

My first instinct was to call for backup, but I hesitated. Who would believe me? I didn't even believe what I was seeing. Instead, I decided to document everything. I pulled out my phone and started taking pictures and recording video. As I moved closer, the creature stirred, and its eyes opened.

The moment our eyes met, I felt a jolt of fear unlike anything I had ever experienced. Its gaze was intelligent, almost human, and filled with pain. It tried to move, letting out a low growl that reverberated through my bones. I backed away slowly, my heart pounding in my chest.

Realizing I needed to get out of there, I hurried back to my cruiser. The sense of vulnerability out in the open was overwhelming. The creature was beginning to stir, and I didn't want to stick around to see what would happen next. I jumped back into the driver's seat, locked the doors, and took a deep breath.

The engine sputtered but eventually roared to life. I reversed carefully, giving the road and surrounding trees a wide berth, and then sped off down the highway. My mind was racing, trying to process what had just happened. I kept glancing in the rear view mirror, half-expecting the creature to be chasing me. But the road remained empty.

The drive home felt like it would never end. My heart was still pounding, and my hands were shaking. I tried to make sense of what I had seen, but it was impossible.

I was the type of idiot who laughed when someone said they believed in Bigfoot. Now I feel bad for mocking people.

When I finally reached home, I parked in the driveway and sat there for a moment, trying to calm my nerves. The house was dark, my family already asleep. I decided not to wake them, not wanting to scare them with my wild tale. Instead, I went inside, locked the doors, and poured myself a stiff drink.

I barely slept that night. Every sound outside my window made me jump, and my mind kept replaying the encounter. The next morning, I reviewed the photos and videos I had taken. They were pretty clear but I have never showed a soul. I don't need that kind of attention.

I debated whether to report the incident or not. As a retired state trooper, I knew how these things could spiral out of control. In the end, I decided to keep it to myself, I didn't want to be ridiculed.

The encounter left me with more questions than answers. What was that creature? Where had it come from? And most importantly, were there more of them out there?

The fear I felt that night never fully went away. I became more cautious, always alert when driving at night or venturing into the woods. My once peaceful hunting trips were now tinged with a sense of unease. Every rustle in the bushes, every forest noise, set my heart racing.

I started carrying more gear, including a high-powered rifle and extra ammunition. I wasn't sure if it would make a difference, but it gave me a sense of security. I also installed motion sensor lights around my property, hoping to deter any unwanted visitors.

Over time, I learned to live with knowing that Bigfoot is real.

BACK ROAD BIGFOOT

KANSAS

I'm Beau, a lifelong resident of Kansas. In a small town where everyone knows each other, life can be pretty straightforward—sometimes to the point of boredom. About five years ago, on a particularly dull evening, my friends and I decided to take a drive out of town to break the monotony. It ended up being an unforgettable night, but not in a good way.

It was late August, and the summer heat was finally starting to break. The stars were out in full force, painting the sky with a brilliance that only the Kansas countryside can provide. We were sitting in Tyson's living room, flipping through channels and struggling to find something to do. Tyson, our unofficial leader, was always up for a bit of adventure, and tonight was no different.

Tyson had an old, beat-up sedan—not exactly built for off-roading, but it was all we had. Matt, Ryan, and I were on board. We piled into the car, with Tyson behind the wheel, Matt riding shotgun, and Ryan and I crammed into the back.

We left town and headed into the darkness, the headlights cutting through the night. Tyson was driving like he always did—fast and carefree, but tonight felt different. The recent heavy rains had left the country roads in bad shape, with deep divots and washouts making the drive more treacherous than usual.

I was sitting in the backseat, trying to enjoy the ride, but every bump and jolt made my stomach flip. The car wasn't built for this kind of terrain, and I was worried Tyson would pop a tire or slide into a ditch. But Tyson's confidence kept us going.

We were about fifteen miles out of town when Tyson decided to take a narrower, more rugged road. It was one of those backroads that probably hadn't seen maintenance in decades. The gravel was loose, and the ruts were deep. The car groaned with every dip and bump, and I could feel the tension in the air.

The road was pitch black, the only light coming from our headlights, casting eerie shadows on the trees that lined the road. We were in the middle of nowhere, miles away from the nearest farmhouse or sign of civilization.

Suddenly, out of nowhere, a large figure appeared in

the beam of the headlights. Tyson slammed on the brakes, and we all lurched forward as the car skidded to a stop. The creature was enormous, probably eight feet tall, covered in shaggy, dark hair. It walked upright on two legs, its long arms swinging at its sides. For a moment, it stood still, caught in the headlights, and then it turned its head and its body to look at us. Its eyes glowed with an eerie red and I couldn't believe my eyes. This was insane.

We were all frozen, too shocked to move or speak. The creature then crossed the road in front of us with a slow, long stride, disappearing into the darkness on the other side.

We all started screaming at Tyson to get out of there. He finally snapped out of it and managed to get the car into reverse. He turned the car around as quickly as he could, the wheels slipping on the loose gravel. We started back the way we came, but we had to go slow to avoid ending up in a ditch or hitting one of the many washouts.

The drive back was excruciating. I kept looking out the rear window, half-expecting the creature to be chasing us. The tension in the car was so thick; nobody said a word.

When we finally made it back to town, we pulled into the first gas station we saw and sat there in silence, the engine ticking as it cooled. We were too stunned to speak, each of us lost in our thoughts, trying to figure out if what we had seen was real.

In the days that followed, we didn't talk about the incident much. We all seemed to understand that sharing it with others would only invite ridicule and disbelief. But the experience left a mark on each of us.

At night, I found it hard to sleep. Every sound outside my window made me jump, and my dreams were filled with images of the creature's glowing eyes and massive frame. I avoided going out after dark.

I was glad to move from that town a few years later and relocate across the country. I haven't spoken to those guys since then. While I know Bigfoots could be anywhere, I prefer to stick to places with more people and avoid driving at night whenever possible.

BIGFOOT CHASED US

I'm Dirk, a lifelong Texan. Growing up in a small northern town where the stars light up the night sky and the plains seem endless, I always appreciated the simple, straightforward life. I never believed in the supernatural—those were just silly stories to me. Well, life proved to me you truly never know what is really out there.

It was a quiet, warm night in late August 2019. My wife, Sarah, and I had just finished dinner at her parents' house. We had spent the evening catching up, sharing stories, and enjoying her mom's famous pot roast. It was a good night, the kind that makes you feel grateful for family and the simple pleasures of life. We said our goodbyes around 9 PM and started the drive back home.

We lived about an hour away, out in the country. The roads were dark and quiet, with only the occasional farmhouse breaking up the vast, empty landscape. As we drove, we talked about the usual things—work, plans for the weekend, and the latest gossip from town. We were in good spirits, laughing and joking, with no idea that our night was about to take a terrifying turn.

We were about halfway home, driving down a particularly isolated stretch of road, when it happened. The night was pitch black, and the only light came from our headlights cutting through the darkness. Suddenly, out of nowhere, a massive figure appeared at the edge of the road. It moved so quickly that I barely had time to react. I swerved to avoid hitting it, the car skidding on the gravel shoulder.

Sarah screamed, and my heart raced furiously. I managed to bring the car to a stop, and for a moment, everything was unnervingly silent. We sat there, breathing heavily, trying to process what we had just witnessed. I turned to Sarah, her face ashen in the dim light of the dashboard.

Before she could respond, we heard a deep, guttural growl coming from the darkness. I turned my head slowly, and there, standing at the edge of the road, was the largest creature I had ever seen. It was easily eight feet tall, covered head to tall in hair, except its face. It had glowing red eyes and looked mad as hell.

For a few seconds, we were frozen with fear. I couldn't process what was right in front of me. It simply didn't fit with the animals I knew. This couldn't be real. I had always been a skeptic, someone who laughed off stories of Bigfoot and other mythical creatures. But there it was, standing right in front of us.

The creature took a step towards the car, and I snapped out of my trance. I hit the gas, the tires spinning on the gravel before catching and propelling us forward. The creature let out a roar, a sound so primal and terrifying that it shook me to my core. I glanced in the rear view mirror and saw it running after us, its long arms swinging with a frightening speed. This thing was pissed.

We sped down the road, the car bumping and jolting over the uneven surface. Sarah was crying, her hands clutching the seatbelt as if it could somehow protect her. I kept my foot on the gas, my eyes darting between the road ahead and the mirror. The creature was still behind us, gaining ground despite our speed.

Its massive frame moved with a shocking agility, covering the ground in long, powerful strides. The headlights illuminated its face for a brief moment—an ape-like visage with deep-set eyes and a wide mouth full of sharp teeth. Its hair or fur was dark, clinging to its muscular body as it chased us through the night.

I pushed the car harder, the speedometer creeping past 50, then 60 miles an hour. The creature was relentless, its roars echoing through the darkness, making it feel like the night itself was alive and hunting us. The car's engine roared in protest as I floored the accelerator, desperate to put as much distance between us and the creature as possible.

As we approached 65 miles an hour, I glanced back and saw the creature beginning to fall behind. Its strides grew shorter, and its roars became less frequent. Finally, it stopped, standing in the middle of the road, watching us speed away. Its eyes glowed in the rear view mirror, a haunting reminder of how close we had come to a real-life nightmare.

We drove for miles without saying a word, in complete shock. Eventually, the road smoothed out, and the lights of our town appeared on the horizon. The terror of the encounter slowly gave way to disbelief and exhaustion. We pulled into our driveway, our bodies and minds exhausted.

We went inside and didn't even talk about it that night. The next morning, my wife asked me what it was, and all I could say was, "I think it was a Bigfoot." I expected her to laugh, but she just looked down at her feet and took another sip of her coffee. We haven't talked about it since. I'd be willing to, but my wife avoids the subject as much as possible. I guess it was just too terrifying for her, as it certainly was for me. I still can't believe we saw it.

We no longer visit my in-laws' house at night. When they ask why, I make up a story about my poor night vision. Time has helped a little, but I don't think I'll ever forget the look on that grotesque face. I feared for our lives and have no doubt that if it caught us, it would have killed us.

BE CAREFUL WHAT YOU WISH FOR

TEXAS

When I was a kid, my friends and I spent our days exploring the woods, fishing in the creeks, and camping out under the stars. It was a simple, idyllic life, but there was always an undercurrent of something else—something wild and unexplained.

I was ten years old the first time I saw it. It was a hot summer evening, and I was walking home from a friend's house. The sun had just dipped below the horizon, casting long shadows across the road. I took a shortcut through a patch of woods, a path I had walked a hundred times before. But that night was different.

I remember hearing something move through the bushes and feeling very vulnerable all of a sudden. I stopped, and strained to see what was making the noise. At first, I thought it was just a deer, there's plenty in these parts. But when I looked to my left I saw this huge black silhouette standing on two legs and it seemed to be looking right at me.

Lord knows this thing was as big as Shaquille O'Neill and built like him too. Its eyes glowed red that easily stood out in the darkness. I was frozen with fear, unable to move or even scream. The creature just stood there for a minute or so looking me over and then simply turned around and left. Just like that.

I ran home as fast as my legs could carry me, bursting through the front door and babbling incoherently about what I had seen. My parents tried to calm me down, but I could tell they didn't believe me. They chalked it up to an overactive imagination, a product of too many ghost stories and late-night horror movies. But I knew what I had seen, and it haunted me for years.

As I grew older, my fascination with the creature only deepened. I devoured books and documentaries about Bigfoot, scouring the internet for any scrap of information I could find. By the time I was in my twenties, I had become a full-fledged "squatcher," dedicating my weekends to searching the woods for any sign of the elusive creature.

I wasn't alone in my obsession. My two best friends,

Dwayne and Cam, shared my passion for the unknown. We spent countless hours hiking through the forests of East Texas, setting up trail cameras, and analyzing footprints. It was thrilling, a real-life adventure that made us feel like explorers on the brink of a monumental discovery.

It was a chilly October weekend when we set out on what would become our last expedition. The leaves were just beginning to turn, and the air was a little cool. We had heard rumors of recent sightings in a remote area of the Piney Woods, a dense and sprawling forest that stretched for miles. Armed with our cameras, audio recorders, and plenty of supplies, we were determined to finally capture undeniable proof of the creature's existence.

We hiked deep into the woods, far from any trails or roads. The forest was quiet, save for the distant call of a bird. As the sun began to set, we found a small clearing and set up camp. We built a fire, cooked a simple meal, and settled in for the night, our eyes and ears alert for any sign of movement.

It was around midnight when we first heard it—something large walking just outside of the fire light. We froze, our hearts pounding out of our chests. Dwayne grabbed his flashlight and shone it into the trees, but the beam was swallowed by the inky blackness. The foot falls continued, louder and closer this time.

Without warning, there was a loud crash as something enormous barreled through the underbrush. We jumped to our feet, adrenaline coursing through our veins. I fumbled for my camera, trying to steady my shaking hands. The creature emerged from the shadows, its massive body illuminated by the flickering firelight.

It was even larger than I remembered. It stood on two legs, its broad chest heaving with each breath. For a moment, we were all frozen, too shocked to move or even speak.

Then it roared—a sound so deep and powerful that it seemed to shake the very ground beneath our feet. The creature took a step towards us, its massive hand reaching out. Panic surged through me, and I turned and ran, my friends close behind.

We tore through the woods, branches whipping at our faces and roots threatening to trip us up. The creature was right behind us, its heavy footsteps pounding the earth. I could hear its growls spurring me to run even faster.

We stumbled into a small ravine, the steep sides offering a brief moment of cover. I crouched behind a fallen log, gasping for breath. Dwayne and Cam were beside me, their faces looked like how I felt.

We could hear the creature moving through the trees above us, its growls growing fainter as it moved away. We stayed hidden, too scared to move or even breathe. It felt like hours before we finally dared to climb out of the ravine and make our way back to camp.

When we returned to our campsite, it was a scene of chaos. The fire was out, and our gear was scattered and torn. It was clear that the creature had searched the area after we fled, likely looking for us or food. We quickly gathered what we could and started the long, tense hike back to the car.

The drive home was silent. Each of us was lost in our own thoughts, disappointed in how the hunt went. The terror of that night had shattered our enthusiasm for squatching. The thrill of the hunt was gone, replaced by a deep, abiding fear.

I haven't been back in the woods since that night. The encounter left a scar that time hasn't been able to heal. Dwayne and Cam feel the same way—we've all moved on, not wanting to go anywhere near the woods.

Be careful what you wish for. It's a saying that I've come to understand all too well. We went into the woods seeking adventure, but what we found was something far more terrifying than we could have ever imagined.

BIGFOOT GRABBED MY BOOT

I am from Northern Minnesota and learned to shoot a rifle before I could ride a bike. So, it's no surprise that the woods have always been my second home. There's a peace in the solitude of the forest, a tranquility that settles deep in your bones. However, early one October morning, that peace was shattered in a way I wish I could forget.

It was the first day of the season, and I was up before dawn, the excitement buzzing in my veins like it did every year. I packed my gear—rifle, camouflage, thermos of hot coffee—and headed out to my favorite spot, a secluded part of the forest about a mile from my cabin. There was a light breeze, the ground covered in a light frost that crunched under my boots.

I reached my tree stand just as the first light of dawn was creeping over the horizon. The stand was perched about 15 feet up an old oak tree, giving me a perfect view of the clearing below. I settled in, wrapped myself in my camouflage jacket, and waited. The forest was waking up around me, the sounds of birds and the noise of small animals filling the air.

I was sitting there, sipping my coffee and watching the sun rise, when I heard something unusual. It was a soft shuffling, different from the normal sounds of the forest. I froze, listening intently. The noise was getting closer, and whatever it was, it was big. I strained my eyes, peering through the early morning light, but I couldn't see anything.

Then, out of nowhere, a massive figure stepped into the clearing. It was walking on two thick hairy legs, and it shocked me to my core. It was part beast and part man or ape, I guess. I'd heard stories of Bigfoot, or Sasquatch, but those things weren't real. Yet here it was, real as anything, and it was heading straight for my tree.

The creature moved with a strange grace for something so large. I am guessing it was at least nine feet tall, with the widest shoulders you could imagine and jacked up like a body builder. As it got closer, I could see its face—an unsettling mix of human and ape-like features, with huge black eyes.

I couldn't move if i wanted to. I was paralyzed with fear,

my hands gripping my rifle so tight. The creature came to the base of my tree and looked up. For a moment, we locked eyes, and I almost lost all control of my bowels. Then, slowly, it reached up and wrapped its massive hand around my boot.

I didn't dare move. The creature gave my boot a gentle tug, almost like it was curious. But there was an anger in its eyes, a smoldering rage that made me question if it was going to pull me out of the tree stand. It sniffed the air, its nostrils flaring, and let out a very low, rumbling growl. I could feel the vibration through the tree, and it took everything I had not to scream.

After about 20 seconds, the creature released my boot and stepped back. It looked around the clearing, its eyes scanning the trees as if searching for something. Then, just as silently as it had appeared, it turned and walked away, disappearing into the forest.

I sat there, too terrified to move. Was it real? Had I really just come face-to-face with a Sasquatch? My rational mind struggled to make sense of it, but the fear was all too real.

I stayed in that tree stand for four hours, too scared to come down. Every noise had me on edge, my heart pounding in my chest.

Finally, as the sun climbed higher in the sky and the forest around me came to life, I summoned the courage to climb down. My legs were stiff and shaky from sitting so long, and my hands were still trembling as I packed up my gear. I kept my rifle close, my eyes scanning the trees for any sign of the creature.

The walk back to my cabin was the longest mile I've ever walked. I jumped at every sound, my senses on high alert. I kept expecting the creature to appear again, to come crashing through the trees. But the forest was calm and quiet, the morning's encounter feeling like a distant nightmare.

When I finally reached my cabin, I locked the door behind me and sank into a chair, my mind still reeling. I poured myself a stiff drink, hoping to calm my nerves. It took a few more drinks to have an effect.

Over the next few days I wondered if the creature was just curious, or was it warning me to stay away? The questions were endless, and the answers elusive.

I found it hard to go back into the woods after that experience. I forced myself to go hunting again, but I was always on edge, my senses heightened, waiting to see that thing again.

Eventually, I made a decision. I wouldn't go back to that part of the forest alone. The risk was too great, the fear too overwhelming. I'd find new hunting grounds, places where I could feel safe again. It wasn't an easy choice, but it was the only one that made sense.

KENTUCKY HUNTERS ENCOUNTER BIGFOOT

I was born and raised in Kentucky and I'd have it no other way. Around here, hunting is more than just a pastime—it's a way of life. I've been hunting since I was a boy, and now that I'm in my forties, it's something I get to share with my 12 year old son, Luke. I was excited to take him out hunting for his first big buck but God had other plans for us that day.

We set out well before dawn, the sky still ink-black and the air cool with a bite that made our breath fog up in front of us. Luke was excited, chattering away quietly as we made our way through the underbrush to one of our favorite hunting spots. I could hear the crunch of leaves under our boots and the occasional snap of a twig, but otherwise, the forest was silent.

We had our eyes on a big buck I'd spotted a few days earlier. I'd been tracking it, noting its trails and the times it came to graze. Luke was eager to get his first real prize, and I was looking forward to that proud moment when he'd bag his first deer.

As we settled into our spot, a strange feeling crept over me. Something wasn't right. I couldn't put my finger on it at first, but then I noticed it—a smell that made your eyes water. It was rank, a mix of rotting meat and something else, something wild and earthy. Luke noticed it too, wrinkling his nose and looking at me with wide eyes.

"Dad, what's that smell?" he whispered, his voice trembling slightly.

"I don't know, son," I replied, trying to keep my voice steady. "But stay close and keep quiet."

We stayed there, waiting in silence, the smell growing stronger with each passing minute. Then, just as the first light of dawn began to filter through the trees, we saw it. At first, it was just a shadow moving between the trunks but then it came to the edge of the forest and stood absolutely still.

I couldn't believe what my eyes were seeing and I instantly felt fear. Not just for myself but more so for my son. I m his father and its my job to protect him but if this thing attacked us I would not be able to do a darn thing. It was enormous.

Some say they look human but this thing was anything but. It was more animal-like, its face looked like it was scrunched up with the widest mouth I had ever seen. It had a nose like a human boxer has, all flat but its eyes looked too big for its face. If you asked me to describe it in one word, I would simply say monster. It had minimal hair on its face but a longer beard that hung down to its chest. No neck to speak of and its body was just pure muscle.

This thing could have easily been 9 feet tall and our deer rifles would have only pissed it off if we were stupid enough to take a shot.

The smell was overpowering now, and I could see Luke's eyes watering from it.

We watched in horror as the creature moved with a surprising grace for something so large. It crouched low, and that's when we saw the deer—a big buck we'd had our eye on. The creature moved with lightning speed, grabbing the deer and taking it down with a single, brutal motion. The sound of the deer's neck snapping echoed through the clearing, and I felt a cold wave of fear wash over me.

We were frozen, unable to move or make a sound, as the creature slung the deer over its shoulder like it weighed nothing. It stood there for a moment, its eyes scanning the surroundings as if checking for any threats. Then, without a second glance, it turned and walked back into the bush, disappearing into the thick undergrowth with a grace that belied its size.

I've faced my fair share of danger in the woods, but nothing like this. My heart was pounding so hard I thought it might burst, and I could see the terror in Luke's eyes. We remained still for a few moments, ensuring the creature was truly gone. The forest seemed to hold its breath, acknowledging the presence of something that shouldn't exist.

We managed to put some distance between us and the creature, moving as quickly and quietly as we could. Once we were far enough away, we broke into a run, not stopping until we were back at the truck. We both tumbled inside, slamming the doors and locking them, breathing hard and shaking from the adrenaline.

"Dad, what was that?" Luke asked, his voice trembling with fear.

"I don't know, son," I replied, my own voice shaking. "But we're not going back there. Not ever."

I still hunt, and so does Luke, but we're more on edge now. We never go out alone, and we always keep an eye on our surroundings. The woods are still a place of beauty and peace, but we know now that there's something out there, something I never thought was possible.

BIRD WATCHER'S UNFORGETTABLE MORNING

MARYLAND

Hey there, my name is Carol, and I'm a 54-year-old woman from Maryland. I'm an avid birder—a passionate bird watcher—and my husband and grown son encouraged me to share this encounter. It happened one early morning, around 6:45 a.m., when I was out for my usual walk around Oxbow Lake. What started as a routine bird-watching trip turned into something that still scares me whenever I think about it

It was a beautiful spring morning. The sun was shining, and the air was perfectly still. As soon as I set foot on the trail, I knew something was off. I just had a feeling. Normally, the early morning is a symphony of bird calls, chirping, and rustling as wildlife starts its day. But that day, there was nothing. Not a single bird song or call. No deer, no squirrels, nothing. The silence was unsettling, almost oppressive.

I paused to take it all in. No birds, no frogs, not even the peepers. Complete and utter silence. As a birder, I can tell you this is highly unusual. Oxbow Lake is typically alive with activity, especially in the early hours. The absence of sound felt unnatural.

As I continued along the trail, I reached a spot where I usually see deer. Again, nothing. But then, I noticed a strange odor. It was a strong, musky smell—not like a dog or a skunk, but something else entirely. I've spent countless hours in the woods, and this was a smell I had never encountered before. It was heavy and oppressive, lingering in the air and making me feel uneasy.

While I stood there, trying to figure out where the smell was coming from, something happened that defied all logic. About 100-150 feet away, a live tree, easily 30-40 feet high, just fell. There wasn't even a hint of a breeze that day. I've spent my childhood in the deep woods of the Adirondack Mountains, and I know trees don't just fall for no reason. It went against everything I understood about nature.

As I stood there, stunned, I felt it—a piercing sensation of being watched. It wasn't just a feeling; it was an intense awareness that something was staring at me. It dawned on me that the tree might have been pushed as a warning. My instincts screamed at me to leave.

I decided it was time to head back to my car. The silence still hung heavily in the air, and I could feel my pulse quicken with every step. Just before reaching my car, I went to an overlook to take one last look at the lake. That's when I heard it—a loud howling from the opposite side of the lake. It echoed through the marsh area, deep and resonant. There were three or four howls, each one creepy as hell. Then, as suddenly as it had started, the silence returned.

I walked back to my car, confused, and drove home shaking my head. My husband and son listened as I recounted the experience, but even as I spoke, it felt surreal. The smell, the silence, the tree, the howls—it just didn't make sense.

Since that day, I've thought a lot about what happened. I've tried to rationalize it, to fit it into my understanding of the natural world, but it just doesn't. Whatever it was, it felt intelligent. It wasn't just an encounter; it was a message. And it's one I won't soon forget.

HIKING GROUP FINDS STRUCTURES

Hi, I'm Penny, a 34-year-old from Maryland, and I've always loved hiking. The beauty of the outdoors, the fresh air, and the thrill of exploring new trails have always been my thing. I've been part of a hiking group for years now, and we usually stick to our favorite paths. But one late April day, we decided to mix things up and take a different route. What a mistake that was!

It was an overcast day, with the sky covered in a blanket of gray clouds that made everything look a bit eerie but also serene. We were a group of six—my friends Jenny, Lionel, Lisa, Tim, and Nicky. Spirits were high, and we were all enjoying the cool, clean air as we made our way through the woods. The ground was damp from the recent rains, and the earthy smell of wet leaves and soil filled the air.

About an hour into our hike, we came across a small open area we had never seen before. In the middle of this clearing were several tall stick structures, standing like silent sentinels. They were roughly built, almost like giant bird nests made from branches and leaves. We were intrigued, to say the least. We had never seen anything like it on our usual trails.

"Look at this," Lionel said, pointing to one of the structures. "What on earth could they be?"

"Maybe some kind of shelter?" Jenny suggested, her curiosity piqued.

We approached the structures cautiously. Up close, they were even more impressive, standing about eight to ten feet tall, with intricate weaving of sticks and branches. It was clear they hadn't been made by accident. One of the structures had an opening, and Tim, being the youngest of us all, decided to crawl inside.

"Hey, be careful," Lisa warned, but Tim just waved her off with a grin.

Inside, it was surprisingly spacious. Tim crouched down and looked around. "Guys, this looks like a bedding area," he said, his voice echoing slightly in the enclosed space. There were leaves and moss arranged in a way that suggested something—or someone—had been sleeping there. Inside, it smelt musty mixed with a wet dog smell.

As we stood there, a strange feeling began to creep over us. The excitement of discovery was quickly replaced by a sense of unease. It felt like we were intruding on something private, something we weren't supposed to see.

"Do you guys feel that?" Nicky asked, her voice barely above a whisper. "Like we're not welcome here?"

I nodded, a chill running down my spine. "Yeah, I feel it too. Maybe we should head back."

We agreed and started making our way back the way we came. That's when the hoots started. At first, they were distant, echoing through the trees like some kind of eerie bird call. But as we continued walking, they got closer and more frequent. It wasn't long before the first rock was thrown. It landed with a thud a few feet away from us, making us all jump.

"What the hell was that?" Lionel exclaimed, looking around frantically.

"Keep moving," I urged, my heart skipping a beat. "Let's just get out of here."

As we quickened our pace, the hoots grew louder, and more rocks were thrown. It was clear we were being followed. Then Tim, who had been inside the structure, started to panic. He took off running, his footsteps pounding on the forest floor.

"Tim, wait!" Lisa shouted, but he didn't stop.

We all broke into a run, trying to keep up with Tim. My breath was coming quick, and my legs felt like they were made of lead. The hoots were now accompanied by low growls, that sent terror straight through me. I could hear rocks crashing through the trees, some landing alarmingly close.

We finally reached the main trail, our hearts about to explode. Tim was already there, bent over and gasping for breath. We didn't stop until we reached our cars, the sense of relief washing over us like a wave. We jumped into our vehicles, not caring about the mud we tracked in, and sped off.

We didn't talk much on the drive back. The fear and adrenaline were still coursing through our veins. When we finally did speak, it was in hushed tones, as if speaking louder might somehow bring the terror back.

"What do you think that was?" Nicky asked, her voice trembling.

"I have no idea," I replied, shaking my head. "But it definitely didn't want us there."

Since that day, we've all been hesitant to take unknown trails. The memory of those hoots and the feeling of being watched still linger in our minds. We stick to the well-trodden paths now, and we always make sure we're back before dark. None of us ever went back to that clearing, and I don't think we ever will.

RABBIT CALLS AND HOWLS

TENNESSEE

Hey y'all, my name's Jimmy, and I'm a country boy through and through. There ain't much out here that scares me, but let me tell you about one night a few years back that still makes my skin crawl just thinkin' about it.

It was a clear, chilly night in late fall, with a few clouds overhead. My buddy Hal and I decided we'd head out to this open field, about an acre wide, to try and call up some coyotes. We had this wounded rabbit call that usually did the trick, bringin' them in for a closer look.

We parked Hal's old truck at the edge of the field and set up camp. We were sittin' there in the dark, just listenin' to the night sounds, waitin' for the coyotes to show up. I had my rifle ready, and Hal was workin' the call, makin' it sound like a rabbit in distress.

After a while, we started hearin' somethin' movin' around in the woods. At first, we figured it was just a coyote or maybe a deer, but then the sounds got louder and closer. It sounded like whatever it was, it was movin' towards us, but it wouldn't step out into the light of the field.

Suddenly, this godawful noise erupted from the darkness. It was a two-toned sound, somewhere between a roar and a cry, louder than anythin' I'd ever heard. I've been inside the lion house at feedin' time, and let me tell ya, those lions didn't have nothin' on this thing.

This thing let out about 12 to 15 cries, each one makin' my heart pound harder in my chest. It was a gut-wrenchin' sound, full of anger or pain or somethin' else I couldn't quite put my finger on. Whatever it was, it was upset, and it wasn't happy about us bein' there.

Hal and I just sat there, frozen, listenin' to this creature cryin' out from the darkness. It was movin' around, but it wouldn't come into the light. I tried to get a fix on it with my flashlight, a powerful 100,000 candlepower beam, but I couldn't see a thing. The sound was comin' from about 120 feet away, but it might as well have been right next to us.

After the cries stopped, there was a silence that felt like it would never end. The only thing I could hear was my own heartbeat and the sound of Hal breathin' heavily next to me. We didn't dare move, didn't dare make a sound. I started to worry about where this thing was and what it might do next.

I've hunted all my life, been in some pretty hairy situations, but I ain't never felt fear like that before. It was primal, deep in my bones, and I knew we needed to get out of there. I didn't say a word to Hal, just nodded, and we both slowly backed our way to the truck, our eyes dartin' around tryin' to see into the darkness.

We got into the truck and high-tailed it out of there, gravel flyin' as Hal gunned the engine. Neither of us said a word on the drive back, just sittin' in silence, tryin' to process what we'd just experienced. That sound, that terrible cry, kept echoing in my head.

When we finally got back to town, we went our separate ways, too shaken to talk about it. I didn't go back to that field for two weeks. When I did, it was in the middle of the day, and I was lookin' for tracks or any sign of what had made that noise. But there was nothin'. No tracks, no disturbed ground, nothin' to prove that we hadn't imagined the whole thing.

Now, years later, Hal and I don't talk about it much, but when we do, we both agree that it was somethin' not of this world.

A STRANGE WELCOME

Hey y'all, my name's Bob, and I'm a country boy from Tennessee. Now, I ain't never been one to believe in UFO's or tall tales, but I gotta tell ya about somethin' that happened to my wife, Jenny, and me when we moved to Missouri a few years back. This story still makes the hairs on the back of my neck stand up, and I ain't one to scare easy.

Jenny and I had been married for about ten years when we decided to pack up and move to a new semi-rural home in Missouri. Her job was relocatin' us, and the thought of a fresh start sounded good. The house was nice, a bit old-fashioned but had plenty of charm, and it was nestled in some beautiful countryside. We figured it'd be a peaceful place to settle down.

About a month after we moved in, Jenny was outside one sunny afternoon, hangin' clothes on the line. I was inside, tryin' to fix the old creaky door that wouldn't stay shut. She hollered at me to come out, but I was too busy wrestlin' with that door. Later, she told me she thought she saw our neighbor's dog out in the field a few hundred feet away. But somethin' about it wasn't right. She said it moved different, like its front legs were too long.

"Roy, it was the strangest thing," she said when she came back inside. "That dog just didn't look right."

"Probably just a stray," I told her, thinkin' nothin' of it. "This is the country, after all."

A week went by, and things were quiet. Then one evenin', just before dusk, Jenny saw it again. This time, it was up on a hill, and there were two of them. One of 'em stood up on two legs, clear as day. Now, I ain't never seen Jenny so scared. She came runnin' inside, white as a ghost.

"Roy, I saw it again! And it stood up like a person!" she exclaimed, her voice shakin'.

I laughed it off, thinkin' she was just spooked. "You sure you didn't see a bear or somethin'? Bears can stand on their hind legs, you know."

"No, Roy, it wasn't no bear. It was like a dog, but bigger and… just wrong," she insisted.

Jenny, bein' the persistent woman she is, decided to ask

our neighbor about it. The next day, she walked over and struck up a conversation. Mrs. Coppolo was an older lady, been livin' there her whole life. When Jenny mentioned what she saw, Mrs. Coppolo got real quiet.

"Haven't you noticed people don't go outside after dark?" she finally said, givin' Jenny a look that chilled her to the bone.

Jenny came home even more rattled, and I could see the fear in her eyes. I tried to reassure her, but deep down, I was startin' to get a little uneasy myself.

Over the next few months, things got strange. We'd hear noises at night, like somethin' movin' around outside. It was subtle at first—just rustlin' in the bushes or the occasional low growl. But as time went on, the sounds got louder and more frequent. One night, I swore I heard somethin' scratchin' at the back door. I grabbed my shotgun and went to check, but there was nothin' there.

Jenny refused to go outside after dark, and honestly, I couldn't blame her. I started to feel like we were bein' watched, and every little noise set me on edge. Our peaceful countryside home had turned into a place of fear and uncertainty.

Six months after we moved in, Jenny's job relocated us again, and I can't say I was sad to leave. The night before we packed up, I went outside to get some air. The moon was full, and the whole place was lit up like it was daytime. As I stood there, takin' in the quiet, I saw them—those two creatures, standin' on the hill, watchin' our house. They didn't move, just stood there, as if to say goodbye.

I didn't tell Jenny about that last sighting. She was scared enough as it was. We packed up the next day and left, and I couldn't have been more relieved.

Look, I don't know what those things were. Dogs don't stand on their hind legs like people, and I ain't never seen an animal move like that. Some folks might say we imagined it, but I know what we saw. Missouri is a beautiful place, but there's somethin' out there in those hills that I hope I never see again.

A MEMORIAL DAY TO REMEMBER

Hey there, folks. Name's Billy Ray, and I've lived in the hills of Virginia all my life. Now, I've seen some strange things in my time, but what happened on one Memorial Day a few years back still gives me the heebie-jeebies. So, sit back and let me tell you 'bout the day we had a run-in with somethin' I never thought I'd lay eyes on.

It was Memorial Day, and we had the whole family over for a big ol' BBQ. We own a plot of land that's been in the family for generations, and it's perfect for get-togethers. We got a big open field where we set up the grill and tables, and a thick patch of woods with trails perfect for ridin' quad bikes.

Now, the kids were excited as all get-out to get on them quads. My boy, Jimmy, and his cousins were revvin' their engines, ready to tear up the trails. It was a beautiful day, sun shinin', birds chirpin', and the smell of burgers and hot dogs cookin' in the air. Nothin' could go wrong, or so we thought.

The kids took off on their quad bikes, laughin' and hollerin' as they disappeared into the woods. Us grown-ups were sittin' around, shootin' the breeze and enjoyin' the day, when suddenly, we heard a commotion. I looked up and saw two of the boys comin' back, one of 'em ridin' on the back of the other's quad, lookin' worse for wear.

Jimmy was the one on the back, and he was a sight. His face was all bruised up, and there was blood tricklin' down his forehead. I jumped up and ran over, my heart poundin' in my chest.

"Jimmy! What in tarnation happened?" I hollered.

Jimmy, his voice all shaky, said, "Pa, we were racin' through the trail when somethin' big came outta the brush and clipped the back of my quad. I got flung into the bushes, and my quad crashed. Thank God, Johnny was right behind me and picked me up."

Johnny, his eyes wide as saucers, added, "Uncle Billy, it was a Bigfoot! I saw it clear as day! It was huge, covered in hair, and it just came outta nowhere!"

Now, I ain't one to believe in fairy tales and monsters,

but the look in their eyes told me they'd seen somethin' real. Jimmy was shakin' like a leaf, and Johnny wasn't much better. An icy wave washed over me, and my gut told me they weren't makin' this up.

I helped Jimmy off the quad and checked him over. He was banged up pretty good, but nothin' seemed broken. We got him cleaned up and bandaged, but the boys were too rattled to talk much more about what happened. They just kept sayin' it was a Bigfoot and that it came outta the brush and knocked Jimmy right off his quad.

After makin' sure Jimmy was alright, a few of us men decided to go check out the spot where it happened. We grabbed our rifles, just in case, and headed down the trail the boys had been racin' on. The woods were thick, and the sunlight barely filtered through the trees, givin' everything an eerie feelin'.

We reached the spot where Jimmy's quad had crashed. It was turned over, and there were broken branches and disturbed brush all around. But what really caught our attention were the tracks. Big, deep impressions in the dirt, too big for a human. They were huge, easily twice the size of a man's foot, and they led off into the woods.

"Holy moly, look at these tracks," my brother-in-law, Pete, said, his voice barely above a whisper.

"Whatever made these wasn't no bear," I replied, my voice tinged with unease.

We followed the tracks a little ways, but the further we went, the more unsettled we felt. The woods were silent, like all the animals had taken off. After a while, we decided it was best to head back and not press our luck. Whatever it was, it didn't seem like a good idea to go lookin' for it.

When we got back, we told the rest of the family what we'd seen. The kids were still shaken up, and the adults were pretty spooked too. We decided to cut the BBQ short and call it a day. Everyone packed up and headed home, leavin' us with more questions than answers.

Jimmy and Johnny didn't talk much about what happened after that. They were traumatized, and it took a while for them to get back on the quads. Even then, they stuck close to home and avoided that trail.

I ain't never seen a Bigfoot myself, but I believe my boy and his cousin. Whatever it was, it was real enough to scare the daylights outta them and leave tracks that none of us could explain. We've owned that plot of land for years, and nothin' like this ever happened before.

I still think about that Memorial Day every now and then. We've had plenty of family get-togethers since, but we always keep a close eye on the kids, and we don't venture too far into those woods.

If you have an encounter you would like
to share, please email me at <u>lukatjacobs@
gmail.com</u>. You can remain anonymous.

AUTHOR BIO

Luka T. Jacobs is an author with a passion for cryptids, particularly Sasquatch and Dogman. Originally hailing from Sydney, Australia, Luka now calls the picturesque Illawarra region of New South Wales home, where she resides with her partner and their cheeky little dog, Finnigan.

With a deep love for animals and a keen sense of adventure, Luka's fascination with the mysteries of the natural world fuels her storytelling. Drawing from her background in Graphic Design and Art, she brings a unique visual flair to her writing.

As an avid traveler and explorer of the unknown, Luka continues to seek inspiration from the wild and untamed corners of the world, eager to share her imaginative worlds with readers everywhere.

Facebook: https://www.facebook.com/lukatjacobs

Amazon: https://www.amazon.com/stores/ Luka-T-Jacobs/author/B0CYW9MCG7

Website: https://www.lukatjacobs.com

THEY OWN THE NIGHT SNEAK PEAK – CHAPTER 2: CREEPING SENSE OF FEAR

A few days later, after noting that not much had happened, I was awoken at around 2 a.m. by what I thought were bird calls. They sounded like galahs, but there was something off—more mechanical, almost like a recording. As I lay there, trying to shake off the sleep, I realised that someone, or something, was mimicking the bird sounds. But why? It was the middle of the night, and even though I had grown up on a semi-rural property, I had never heard galahs at this hour before.

One call came from behind our house and was answered by another near the barn.

I lay in bed, listening intently for about twenty minutes. Curiosity mingled with a creeping sense of fear. If these sounds were being made by people, they were on our property without permission. The thought that they might know Ted wasn't home and that I was alone with the kids unsettled me. I tried to reassure myself that the house was locked up tight and eventually drifted back to sleep.

The next morning, as I was about to put a load of washing out on the line, I stepped out the back door and headed down the steps. That's when I noticed the footprints in the soil next to the stairs. These were no ordinary footprints. They were massive.

My heart raced as I followed the trail. The footprints circled around the left side of the house and led to the steps at the front of the porch. I stood there, hands on my hips, staring at them, when a strange sensation tickled the back of my neck and shot down my spine. I looked up, my head swiveling, but I couldn't see anyone. Still, I felt eyes on me.

Feeling vulnerable even in broad daylight, I hurriedly hung out the laundry, constantly glancing over my shoulder. I had never seen footprints that big before, and they were bare feet. If there had been teenagers making those bird calls last night, wouldn't they be wearing shoes? No way would I be out at night without shoes, especially in a place where you could easily step on a snake or a sharp rock. But then again, kids were known for acting without thinking.

Besides, we lived out in the boondocks, with our nearest neighbour at least 2 klms away. It wasn't like there were kids up and down the block.

Suddenly I remembered the figure on the barn roof, the bird noises from the night before, and now these footprints. A rising sense of unease washed over me. What the heck was going on here? Did someone want us out of this place, or was I just going crazy?

As I walked back into the house, my mind raced with possibilities. I decided it was time to talk to Ted about everything that had been happening, even if he might brush it off again. The kids were already up, eating breakfast, oblivious to the strange events unfolding around them.

I called Ted, needing to share my growing unease. "Hey, can you talk?" I asked as soon as he answered.

"Sure, what's up?" he replied.

I took a deep breath and recounted everything—the figure on the barn roof, the mechanical bird calls, and the massive footprints. There was a long pause on the other end of the line.

"Look, it's probably just some local kids playing a prank," Ted finally said. "You know how they can be, especially if they hear there's a new family in the area."

"But Ted," I insisted, "the footprints were huge and barefoot. And the noises at night... it didn't sound like kids. And who would walk around here without shoes?"

"I don't know," he said, sounding more thoughtful. "Maybe it's just some kind of local wildlife we're not familiar with. Or an animal with unusual behavior. There could be a logical explanation."

"But what about the figure on the barn roof?" I pressed. "That wasn't an animal."

"You're right," he admitted. "I don't have a good explanation for that. If it happens again, call the police. I will be home in a few days," he finally said. "In the meantime, keep the doors and windows locked. Don't go outside at night."

"Okay," I agreed, feeling a bit more reassured but still uneasy. "Just hurry home, please."

"I will," Ted promised. "You will be ok."

As I hung up the phone, the sense of unease lingered, but knowing Ted would be home soon gave me some comfort. I wasn't 100% sure that he believed me, maybe he just heard the tone in my voice and knew I was genuinely scared. I wasn't normally an emotional person.

I tried to go about my day, but the unease lingered. I couldn't shake the feeling that something was watching us, something that didn't belong in our world. The kids were already up, eating breakfast, oblivious to the strange events unfolding around them.

That night, I stayed up late, making sure all the doors and windows were securely locked. I eventually fell asleep in the early hours and had my first decent sleep in days.

CHAPTER 3: HAND PRINT

The next few days passed uneventfully, but the sense of being watched never left me. I was constantly on edge, jumping at every little sound. Ted tried to reassure me over the phone, but I could tell he was just as unsettled.

Finally, Ted returned home. The relief I felt seeing him walk through the door was overwhWhittakering. I threw my arms around him, holding on tightly, as if afraid he might disappear. He hugged me back, sensing my fear.

"You need to feel safe in your own home," he said firmly. "I'll set up security cameras around the property tomorrow."

That night, as we sat in the living room discussing our plan, a loud thud echoed from outside. My heart leaped into my throat. Ted grabbed a flashlight and stood up, ready to investigate.

"Please, be careful," I whispered, my voice barely audible over the pounding of my heart.

He nodded and headed out the door. I watched from the window, my hands pressed against the glass, eyes straining to see through the darkness. The beam of his flashlight cut through the night, illuminating the path to the barn. Every second felt like an eternity as I waited, my mind racing with worst-case scenarios.

Ted moved cautiously, the flashlight beam dancing across the ground. He scanned the area around the barn but then paused by the car. I saw him lean in, peering closely at something on the driver's side window. He straightened up, his face pale in the moonlight, and hurried back to the house.

"What did you find?" I asked, my voice shaking.

Ted locked the door behind him and took a deep breath. "There's a huge hand print on the driver's side window," he said quietly. "It's too dark to get a good look at it now. I'll check it out properly in the morning."

We stood there for a moment, the gravity of his words sinking in. Something—or someone—was out there, watching us, and it wasn't going away.

The next morning, Ted and I went outside to check the hand print on the window. As it was winter, there was still some frost on the windows, but you could clearly see the hand print in the daylight. It was enormous—at least 2.5 times the size of Ted's hand, and Ted stood at 6'2". The print had a greasy feel to it, unlike anything we had ever encountered.

Ted spent the afternoon setting up cameras around the property, focusing on the areas where we had seen the footprints and heard the noises. As he worked, I couldn't shake the feeling that we were being watched, that unseen eyes were on us, observing our every move. Maybe I was just being paranoid?

I sat on the porch, helping Ted whenever he needed it, while making sure the kids stayed inside. It bothered me to keep them indoors since we had moved here to give them more time outside in the fresh air, yet here we were, telling them not to come outside. They were curious but content to get more free time on their devices.

"Ted, do you think the cameras will catch anything?" I asked, trying to keep my voice steady.

He looked up from adjusting a camera. "I hope so," he said, wiping sweat from his brow. "At the very least, it might give us some answers—or at least some peace of mind."

We continued setting up the cameras, each movement deliberate and careful. The sun began to set, casting long shadows across the yard. The sense of being watched never left me, and I could tell Ted felt it too.

That night, as we reviewed the setup and made sure everything was working, we both felt a glimmer of hope. Maybe, just maybe, we would finally understand what was haunting our new home and take steps to protect our family.

We went to bed feeling a bit more secure, knowing we would at least have some way of seeing what was out there. But deep down, I couldn't shake the feeling that we were dealing with something beyond the ordinary. I opened the security camera app on my phone and watched the footage while Ted snored beside me. He was due to go back out on a run in a weeks time, and I hoped whatever or whoever was outside would move on by then.

As I lay there in bed, I couldn't help but wonder if some-one—or something—wanted us gone. The thought lingered in the back of my mind, refusing to be dismissed.

We had come here seeking peace and a fresh start, but it seemed that the farmstead had other plans for us. And as much as I wanted to believe otherwise, the unsettling feel-ing that we were not alone remained.

Dear Reader,

Thank you for selecting my book from the myriad of options available. Your choice to explore my work is deeply appreciated, and your support means the world to me.

If you've found the book enjoyable, I would be grateful for your help in sharing it with others and leaving a review.

As a self-published author, reviews and word-of-mouth recommendations are vital for reaching new readers and spreading the book's message to a broader audience.